ASPCA kids

PET RESCUE CLUB

A New Home for Truman
No Time for Hallie
Too Big to Run

Written by **Catherine Hapka**
Illustrated by **Dana Regan**

studio
INTERNATIONAL

Cover Illustration by Steve James

Studio Fun International
An imprint of Printers Row Publishing Group
A division of Readerlink Distribution Services, LLC
10350 Barnes Canyon Road, Suite 100, San Diego, CA 92121
www.studiofun.com

Library of Congress Cataloging-in-Publication Data is available on
request.

ISBN 978-0-7944-4254-5
Manufactured, printed, and assembled in Shaoguan, China.
SL/02/18
22 21 20 19 18 1 2 3 4 5

**5-7% of the purchase price will be donated to the ASPCA®, with a
minimum donation of $50,000 through December 2019.**

Table of Contents

WE ARE THEIR VOICE.®

The American Society for the Prevention of Cruelty to Animals® (ASPCA®) was the first humane society to be established in North America and is, today, one of the largest in the world.

The organization was founded on the belief that animals are entitled to kind and respectful treatment at the hands of humans and must be protected under the law. The ASPCA®, headquartered in New York City, provides animal welfare services and programs that extend their anti-cruelty mission across the country, along with helping animals find safe and loving homes.

To learn more, please visit www.aspca.org

A New Home for Truman

For all the shelter workers
who help people find their pets and pets find their people.

—*C. H.*

1

The Best Birthday Ever!

"Happy birthday, Janey!" Lolli Simpson exclaimed.

Janey Whitfield set down her lunch tray at her usual spot across from Lolli. "It's not my birthday yct," she told her best friend with a smile. "Not until tomorrow, remember?"

"I know." Lolli pushed a lock of curly black hair out of her eyes. "But tomorrow is Saturday. I wanted you to be able to celebrate here at school with all your friends."

Lolli waved a hand at the other people

sitting at the table. Their friend Adam Santos was next to Janey. Several kids from their fourth grade class were a little farther down, talking about that morning's spelling test.

"Come on, everybody!" Lolli called out. "Let's sing!"

She led the whole table in a round of "Happy Birthday to You." A few kids at nearby tables joined in. Janey loved every second of it. It was great having everyone sing to her!

"Thanks, everybody!" she called out when the song finished. She waved, and some of the other kids waved back. Soon they all went back to their own conversations. "Thanks, Lolli," Janey told her friend. "That was fab." Janey loved to use interesting words whenever she could. Her favorite right then was "fab." It was short for fabulous.

"Wait—there's more." Lolli reached into her insulated lunch bag and pulled out a small reusable container. Lolli's parents liked to call themselves back-to-the-land hippies. They lived on a small farm outside of town and grew their own organic food. They bought most of their clothes at thrift stores and recycled everything. Lolli never brought brown paper bags or plastic baggies for her lunch like most of the other kids. She had a whole set of reusable bags and containers that she used instead.

"What is it?" Janey opened the container and peered at the grayish-brown lump inside.

"It's a cupcake." Lolli grinned. "Dad helped me make it just for you."

"Oh. Thanks." Janey smiled. "Um, it

looks…interesting."

"That's a cupcake?" a new voice exclaimed loudly in Janey's ear.

Janey looked up. Zach Goldman had just stopped by their table. Zach was friends with Adam, but Janey didn't like him very much.

He was rowdy, loud, and kind of obnoxious. Once when Janey had received the highest grade in the class on a math test, Zach had called her "Brainy Janey" for almost a month.

Zach leaned over for a better look at the cupcake. He was holding his skateboard under his arm, and the end of it poked Janey in the back.

"Ow," she said, pushing him away. "What are you doing?"

Zach grinned. "That doesn't look like a cupcake," he said. "It looks like something one of my mom's patients barfed up."

"Gross!" Janey made a face. Zach's mom was a veterinarian. She treated most of the cats and dogs in town.

"It's a special recipe my dad made up," Lolli told Zach. "With zucchini, kale, and oatmeal. The cupcakes are actually really healthy, and totally organic, too."

"Zucchini and kale?" Zach said. "Do me a favor, Lolli. Don't make me a cupcake on my birthday."

With a grin, he hurried away.

Lolli looked worried. "Does it really look that bad?" she asked Janey. "I ate one of the cupcakes for breakfast, and I thought it was good."

Janey didn't like zucchini. But lots of the food at Lolli's house tasted better than it looked or sounded. So she forced herself to take a tiny bite of her birthday cupcake. She thought it would taste like mud, but it actually wasn't that bad.

"It's great," she said. "I love it. Thanks, Lolli, you're the best friend ever!"

Lolli looked relieved. "No, you are," she said. "So what are you going to do to celebrate your birthday tomorrow?"

That made Janey's smile get even bigger. "I can't wait until tomorrow," she said. "I'm pretty sure Mom and Dad are getting me something really special this year."

"Really? What?" Lolli was digging into her lunch bag again. While she wasn't looking, Janey nudged Adam. Then she broke off more than half of her cupcake and slipped it to him. She put a finger to her lips, and he nodded.

Adam popped the cupcake into his mouth in one big bite. He chewed and swallowed quickly. Then he gave Janey a thumbs-up.

Janey smiled gratefully. Adam was pretty

skinny, but he ate a lot. And he liked almost everything, including the cafeteria's baked beans. Even Lolli's dog, Roscoe, wouldn't touch those!

Thinking about Roscoe reminded Janey of her big news. She turned back to Lolli. "I think my parents are finally getting me a dog," she said.

Lolli's head snapped up in surprise.

"Huh?" she said. "But your dad is so allergic to animals."

Janey's father's allergies were the reason Janey had never had a pet, even though she was crazy about animals of all shapes and sizes. Whenever Mr. Whitfield was around any creature with fur or feathers, he started wheezing and sneezing. His eyes turned red, and his nose turned redder. He sniffled nonstop. It even happened when he was around Janey's aunt's poodle. Janey had read that poodles weren't supposed to bother people with allergies as much since they didn't shed. But her parents had explained that it didn't really work that way.

"I know. But I figured out a way to compromise," Janey told Lolli. "See, I did some research on the Internet. I found out there are allergy shots for people with animal allergies! Isn't that great?"

"Allergy shots?" Lolli looked uncertain. "You want your dad to get shots so you can have a dog?"

"Uh huh. I printed out some articles about the allergy shots." Janey broke off a tiny piece of cupcake and ate it. "I started leaving them lying around the house about a month ago. I figured that would give Dad plenty of time to talk to his doctor about getting the shots. I also left some pictures and information about my favorite dog breeds."

"Really?" Adam looked up from his lunch. "What breeds did you pick?"

Adam was very interested in dogs. Even though he was only nine, he'd been running his own successful pet-sitting business for over a year. He fed and walked people's dogs for them after school and any other time they needed him. He also helped people train their dogs sometimes. He'd taught Roscoe how to shake hands and balance a dog treat on his nose.

"I was thinking about a Maltese or a papillon," Janey told him. "They both seem really cute and fun. And I thought maybe a small dog like that would mean Dad needs to get the shots less often."

Adam nodded. "I walked a Maltese once. I liked her."

Lolli laughed. "You like every dog you walk, Adam," she said. Then she turned to Janey. "Maybe you don't need a fancy breed. What's wrong with a nice all-American mutt like Roscoe?"

"That would be fine, too. Roscoe is totally fab," Janey said. She meant it, too. Roscoe was a big, lovable goof who had come from the local animal shelter as a puppy. He was part rottweiler, part Labrador retriever, and part who-knew-what. Janey had spent many happy hours at Lolli's place playing fetch with Roscoe, swimming with him in the pond, or just lying in the grass rubbing his belly.

"I bet you could find a dog just as great as Roscoe at the Third Street Animal Shelter," Lolli said. "The dogs and cats there all really need homes. My parents and I go there sometimes to volunteer. Actually, Mom said we might go tomorrow to drop off some homemade dog and cat toys we made last weekend. I could help you look at dogs then if you want."

"That would be awesome," Janey said. "I'll mention it to my parents if they haven't gotten my dog yet. Come to think of it, they might be thinking the same thing. They donate money to the shelter every year." She sighed happily. "Anyway, I don't really care what kind of dog I get. I just can't wait to have one of my very own!"

She'd been dreaming about this day ever since she could remember. Janey had always loved animals—all animals. She read books about dogs, hung cute pictures of cats on her walls, and doodled horses and elephants and rabbits all over the margins of her school notebooks. She loved spending time with Roscoe, Adam's dog-sitting clients, and any other animal that came along. But nothing would compare to having a pet of her very own, to cuddle and snuggle with any time she wanted.

It was going to be so great! She shivered with excitement, wondering how she was ever going to wait until tomorrow.

2
Birthday Surprises

Janey woke up early the next morning. For a second she couldn't remember why she was excited. Then she smiled.

"Happy birthday to me!" she said, jumping out of bed.

She pulled on her bathrobe and raced downstairs. The smell of banana pancakes and bacon greeted her.

"Happy birthday, sweetheart!" Janey's father sang out. He was at the stove with a spatula. "I'm making your favorite breakfast."

"Thanks, Daddy." Janey looked around

the kitchen. There was a pile of wrapped gifts on the counter. None of the packages had air holes that she could see.

But she couldn't see her mother, either. Maybe Mom was out in the garage with the dog, waiting to surprise her.

Then her mother hurried in from the

living room. "Happy birthday, Janey, love!" she said. "How does it feel to be a year older?"

"Fab," Janey said. Her father set a platter of pancakes and bacon in front of her, and Janey helped herself. "I can't wait to see what you got me this year!"

Her parents traded a smile. "We can't wait, either," Janey's father said. "Eat your birthday breakfast, and then you can open your gifts."

Janey loved banana pancakes and bacon. But that morning, she hardly tasted them. She ate as fast as she could.

"Finished!" she said, gulping down some juice. "Time for presents."

Her parents both laughed. "All right," her mother said. "Go ahead, love."

Janey grabbed one of the gifts and shook it. Even if there wasn't a dog in the pile of gifts, maybe the packages contained dog stuff, like a collar and leash or food dishes or dog toys. Now that she thought about it, that made more sense anyway. Then Janey would be all ready to go and pick out her own dog at the shelter. She couldn't wait!

She ripped the paper off the first gift. "Oh," she said in surprise.

There was no collar or leash. No dishes or dog toys, either. Just a shirt with a sparkly collar.

"It's the one you liked at the mall last weekend, remember?" her mother said with a smile.

Janey nodded. She did like the shirt, even if she wasn't that excited about it right now.

But maybe she could wear it to the shelter when she chose her dog.

"Thanks," she said. "Next!"

For a second she thought the next gift was a collar, but then she realized it was a bracelet. Janey opened several more packages after that, but all of them contained non-dog gifts.

Finally there was only one gift left. That had to be the dog gift!

Janey picked it up. "Don't shake that one, sweetheart," her father said.

Janey nodded. She had a bad feeling about this. The shape and weight of the gift didn't seem right for any kind of dog stuff. It was light and rectangular.

She opened it quickly. "Oh," she said. "A tablet computer."

"This model just came out last week." Her father sounded excited. "We knew you'd love it!"

Her mother nodded. "Your laptop is getting old," she explained. "This will be so much better."

"It's already fully loaded, too," her father said. "It's got a great browser, a kid-safe blogging platform, and of course all your favorite games—like Puppy Playtime."

Janey perked up. "Puppy Playtime?" she echoed with a smile. "Yes, I do love that game."

She paused, waiting for her parents to say something else about puppies—like that they were taking Janey to get one! But her father just went on talking about the other software on the tablet.

"What's wrong, love?" Janey's mother interrupted her husband. "You don't look as excited as we expected."

Janey bit her lip. Were her parents teasing her? That didn't seem like them.

"What about my dog?" she blurted out.

"Dog?" Janey's mother traded a look with Janey's father.

"Oh, Janey." Her father shook his head. "Is this about those printouts I found on my desk a couple of weeks ago?"

Janey nodded. "Did you read them? All

you need to do is get a few shots and you won't be allergic to animals anymore!"

"I'm afraid it's not that simple," Janey's mother said. "We looked into the shots once, but the doctor advised against it because your father has mild asthma."

Janey couldn't believe that this was happening. She felt her face turning red. If she didn't get away, she'd start crying or yelling—probably both.

"I...I need to call Lolli," she choked out. "I think she wants me to come to her house."

Her mother looked worried. "Are you sure? We were going to watch a movie, or—"

Mr. Whitfield put a hand on his wife's arm. "It's okay, Janey," he said softly. "Go ahead and call Lolli. We can watch that movie later."

There was no answer on the phone at Lolli's farmhouse, so Janey called Lolli's mom's cell phone. It turned out that the whole family was in the car on their way to the shelter.

"We're just five minutes from your house," Mrs. Simpson told Janey. "We'll swing by and pick you up. I know you love visiting the animals at the shelter."

"Thanks," Janey said.

While her father cleared the breakfast dishes and her mother picked up the wrapping paper from her gifts, Janey ran upstairs to change out of her pajamas. Then she stood in the front hall until she saw the Simpsons' battered old station wagon pull to the curb in front of her house.

"Lolli's parents are here to pick me up,"

she called. "I'll be back in a while."

Ten minutes later, she was walking into the Third Street Animal Shelter with Lolli and her parents. Mr. Simpson was carrying a hemp bag filled with homemade dog and cat toys. Mrs. Simpson had a bag of organic kale from her garden. She'd explained that it was for some pet rabbits that had come into the shelter that week.

The shelter was a one-story brick building tucked between the post office and a florist shop. Inside, the lobby was painted with cheerful murals of cats, dogs, and other animals. The muffled sound of barking came from beyond a door marked Dog Room.

"I expected to come here today," Janey said sadly, staring at that door. "But I thought it would be to pick out my own dog."

Mrs. Simpson put her arm around Janey's shoulder. During the ride over, Janey had told Lolli and her parents what had happened.

A young woman came out from behind the front desk and hurried over. She was in her twenties, with a blond ponytail and a bright smile. "Oh, you brought the toys!" she exclaimed. "Thanks so much—I know the critters will love them."

"You're welcome, Kitty," Mrs. Simpson said.

That made Janey smile. "You work in an

animal shelter, and your name is Kitty?" she asked the young woman.

Kitty laughed. "Actually, it's Kathleen," she said. "But after I smuggled a whole litter of kittens into my room as a kid, my family started calling me Kitty. And I guess it stuck!"

"It's Janey's birthday today," Mr. Simpson told Kitty. "Can she play with some animals to help her celebrate?"

"Of course!" Kitty said. "Go on into the Meet and Greet Room, and I'll bring somebody in for you to play with. Would you prefer cats or dogs?"

"I love both," Janey said. "But I especially like dogs, I guess."

She followed Lolli through a doorway across from the front desk. Inside was a small room with a tile floor. There were benches and beanbag chairs, as well as several scratching posts and a bucket filled with toys and treats.

Soon Kitty returned. She was leading two half-grown puppies. One was a small terrier mix, and the other was a tall, gangly brown dog whose fringed tail never stopped wagging.

"This is Buster, and this is Lyle," Kitty said. "They're both super friendly and playful. Go ahead and wear them out if you can— you'll be doing me a favor!" She laughed and left, pulling the door shut behind her.

"Oh, you're adorable!" Janey exclaimed, falling to her knees and cuddling the puppies. For a second she felt happy, like she always did when animals were around. But she felt sad at the same time. She would

love to take home either Buster or Lyle—or better yet, both of them! But that wasn't going to happen.

"They're so cute!" Lolli exclaimed, giggling as Lyle licked her chin. "I bet Roscoe would love a couple of puppies to play with!"

"Don't even think about it," her mother said with a laugh. "One dog is more than enough for this family."

"Oh, well." Lolli smiled. "At least I can play with them here." She turned to Janey. "That gives me a great idea. Why don't we volunteer here at the shelter together? They let kids help out if their parents sign a form. We could come once or twice a week after school."

"That sounds fun," Janey agreed. "Not as much fun as having my own pet, but better than nothing." She hugged Buster as he wiggled onto her lap. "A puppy would be a lot cuddlier than some stupid old tablet."

"I know," Lolli agreed. "Your tablet sounds cool, though. Does it take pictures? Too bad you didn't bring it with you, or I could take some photos of you with Buster and Lyle."

"Yeah." Janey tickled Buster under his furry chin. "But wait—that gives me a totally fab idea…"

3

Janey's Big Idea

Half an hour later, the Simpsons dropped Janey and Lolli off at Janey's house. Janey rushed inside. "Mom! Daddy!" she yelled. "Where are you?"

Her mother came into the front hall from the kitchen. "Hello, Lolli," she said. "Janey, you look like you're in a better mood than when you left."

"I'm sorry about earlier," Janey said, hurrying over to give her mother a hug. "You too, Daddy," she added as her father wandered in carrying a news magazine. "I loved all my presents, even if none of them is a dog."

"Good, good." Her father looked relieved. "I'm sorry we can't get a pet, sweetheart."

"I know. But listen, I had a great idea that might be the next best thing," Janey said.

Her mother smiled. "Uh-oh," she said. "What is it—a robot dog?"

Lolli giggled. "That definitely sounds like something Janey would invent!"

Janey giggled, too. "Maybe someday. But my great idea does involve technology— namely, my awesome new tablet!" The tablet was still on the table where she'd left it. She hurried over and picked it up. "You said this has a blogging program, right?"

"Yes," her father said. "It's a brand new platform made specifically for bloggers under fourteen. There are all kinds of safety features, and—"

"Perfect," Janey interrupted. "Because that's my idea. I'm going to start a blog! It'll be called, um, Janey's Pet Place, and kids can use it to share cute pictures of their cats and dogs and other pets."

"What a wonderful idea, love!" her mother said.

"I know." Janey smiled. "That way, it'll be like I have all the pets in town around me all the time!" She grabbed Lolli's hand. "Come on, I can't wait—let's go up to my room and figure out how to get started!"

• • • • • • • • • •

An hour later, Janey was feeling both excited and frustrated. "The text we wrote is perfect," she told Lolli, "but it won't do any good if we can't figure out how to get the blog set up the way I want it!"

"I know, right?" Lolli poked at the tablet's on-screen keypad. "If this blog thingy is made for kids, shouldn't it be easy to use?"

Janey pulled the tablet closer again and

tried—again—to load the text into the box she'd just finished creating. It looked really cool, with a border of frolicking puppies and kittens and a background of clouds. But when she hit the enter key, all she got in return was an annoying error message—again.

"Aargh!" she cried. "I want to get it working already so I can start getting cute pet photos!"

A bark drifted in through the window. "Maybe that dog outside wants to be on your blog," Lolli joked. "He's telling you to hurry up!"

Janey hopped off her bed and went to the window. A cute golden retriever was sniffing the bushes along the sidewalk. A familiar figure was holding the dog's leash.

"Hey, it's Adam!" Janey told Lolli. "He's

walking one of his dog-sitting clients. Let's go ask him if he knows how to work the blog software."

"Adam?" Lolli sounded dubious. "He's not that interested in computers—just dogs."

Janey tucked her tablet under her arm and headed for the door. "Still, he's smart, right?" she said. "Maybe he can figure out what we're doing wrong. Besides, I love that golden retriever he's walking right now—I want to go out and pet him."

Lolli smiled. "In that case, what are we waiting for?"

The big, friendly dog greeted Janey and Lolli happily. So did Adam. But he shook his head as he studied the blog screen.

"Sorry, guys," he said. "I have no clue.

Maybe you should ask Zach. He's practically a technology genius."

"Zach? Really?" Now it was Janey's turn to be doubtful. She didn't think Zach was good at anything except being totally obnoxious!

"Uh-huh." Adam bent down to untangle the leash from around the golden retriever's leg. "He helped my parents set up a photo-sharing site last year so my relatives can all see pictures of my little sisters and me. And he's always fixing the computer his dad uses for work. I bet a blogging site will be no problem for him."

"It's worth a try," Lolli said. "Zach lives near here, doesn't he?"

"He's on the next block," Janey said. She frowned at Adam. "Are you sure he's good with computer stuff? What if he wrecks my new tablet?"

"He won't," Adam said. "Trust me, he can get your blog working if anyone can."

Janey sighed. "Fine," she said. "I guess we can go see if he's home. I'd do just about anything to get my blog started!"

4
Going Live

"There he is," Lolli said as the girls turned the corner onto Zach's block.

Janey saw him, too. Zach was in front of his house. He was messing around with his skateboard, trying to get it to jump over a big crack in the sidewalk.

"Hi," Janey said, hurrying up to him. "What are you doing?"

"Learning Chinese," Zach said with a smirk. "What does it look like?"

Janey looked at the house. Loud music was coming out of an open window. "Is someone having a party?"

"Nah, that's just my older brothers." Zach rolled his eyes. "A bunch of their dumb friends came over. They're lucky my dad is the only one home. My mom would never let them play their stupid music so loud."

"Where's your mom?" Lolli asked.

Zach flipped his skateboard up, catching it in one hand. "At work. Her clinic is open on Saturdays."

"Oh." Janey thought it was so cool that Zach's mom was a veterinarian. That was practically her dream job! She didn't say that, though. She figured Zach would probably just make fun of her. "Listen, Adam says you're good at computers…."

She and Lolli told him about all the problems they were having. When Janey held

out her tablet, Zach's eyes lit up.

"Cool!" he exclaimed. "I've been dying to get one of these!" Then his face fell. "I probably won't, though. My parents say one computer is enough for the whole family to share."

"We only have one computer, too," Lolli told him.

Zach grinned. "Yeah, but that's because your parents are weirdos," he teased her.

"They are not!" Janey retorted with a frown.

But Lolli just laughed. "It's okay. Mom and Dad call themselves weirdos all the time. So Zach, do you think you can help us with the blog?"

"Duh, that's easy." Zach sat down on his skateboard with the tablet on his lap. His fingers flew over the keypad.

"What are you doing?" Janey couldn't help being a little nervous. What if Zach broke her new tablet? Then she'd have to wait until she got it fixed to start her blog.

Zach didn't answer for a second. Finally he looked up and grinned. "There," he said, showing Janey the screen. "Is that all you needed me to do?"

Janey gasped. The blog looked perfect! The text was exactly where it was supposed to be. Zach had cropped and resized the photos of cats and dogs Janey had pasted onto the page, too. She hadn't asked him to do that, but the photos looked better, so she didn't complain.

"Awesome!" she said. "Thanks, you really…"

She cut herself off with a gasp. Something was happening on the screen. As Janey stared in horror, the edges of her blog page seemed to peel back. Then a cartoon dinosaur leaped into view and started chomping on the text box!

"Hey!" she cried while Zach started laughing so hard he almost fell off his skateboard. "You did that on purpose, didn't you?"

"No, it must be a virus or something." Zach was laughing so hard he could barely get the words out. "You should see your face, Janey!"

Lolli giggled. "That's pretty funny, Zach," she said. "How'd you do it?"

"I could tell you, but you wouldn't understand." Zach grinned. "Cool, right?"

"No." Janey was still frowning. "Fix it!"

"Okay, okay." Zach rolled his eyes. "Next birthday, make sure you ask for a sense of humor, okay?"

Lolli smiled at Janey. "Come on, it was a little bit funny, right?" Lolli said in her soothing way. "Besides, I'm sure Zach is going to fix it right now. Right, Zach?"

"Right." Zach was already bent over the tablet again.

Janey was tempted to grab it away from him. But she decided to give Zach one more chance.

And ten minutes later, she was glad. Zach got rid of the dinosaur and adjusted a few other things. Now the blog looked perfect!

"There," Zach said, pressing a key on-screen. "You're live. Kids should be able to see the blog now."

"Thanks, Zach!" Janey took her tablet back and smiled at the screen. "I can't wait for the cute pet pictures to start coming in!"

· · · · · · · · · ·

"How's the blog going, sweetheart?" Janey's father asked the next day as Janey helped him clear the lunch dishes.

"Fab." Janey dropped a handful of silverware into the dishwasher. Then she hurried back to the table and picked up her tablet. "People are already posting tons of awesome pictures! This one's my favorite so far."

She scrolled down and showed him a photo of an adorable black-and-white cat leaping at a butterfly. Her father chuckled.

"Very cute," he agreed. He checked his watch. "Ready to head over to Lolli's? I want to be back here before the game starts on TV."

Janey nodded. She'd made plans to spend Sunday afternoon over at Lolli's house so they could write the next blog entry together. Janey was planning to post every few days with her thoughts about animals and anything else she could think of to write about. She was also going to choose her favorite photos in several categories— cutest pet, funniest pose, best action shot, and other stuff like that. She figured that would encourage people to keep sending photos.

It took about ten minutes to drive to Lolli's farm on the edge of town. Soon the Whitfields' car was bumping and jangling up the Simpsons' long gravel driveway. There was an orchard on one side, and a pasture on the other with two goats and a sheep in it. Usually Janey liked to stop and say hello to the animals, but today she just waved at them as the car passed.

"Have fun," her father said as he stopped in front of the Simpsons' two-story, pointy-roofed farmhouse. The wooden porch sagged a little, and a small flock of chickens was pecking at the dandelions growing on the front lawn. It was very different from the Whitfields' tidy suburban home. But Janey thought the farmhouse was beautiful. She and Lolli had helped Mrs. Simpson paint the shutters a gorgeous shade of sky blue. And everywhere she looked, something was blooming.

As Janey climbed out of the car, the front door opened. Roscoe bounded out, barking happily.

"Hey, buddy!" Janey greeted Roscoe as he almost crashed into her.

Lolli was right behind Roscoe. She waved

to Janey's father as he drove away. Then she grabbed Roscoe by the collar and pulled him away from Janey.

"Leave her alone, Roscoe," she said. "You'll make her drop her tablet!"

"Don't worry, I'm holding on tight," Janey said with a laugh. "Ready to see more cute pictures?"

Just then the tablet let out a ping. "Ooh!" Lolli said. "Does that mean someone else just posted a photo?"

"Uh-huh. We should try to guess what kind of animal it will be this time," Janey said, holding her hand over the screen. "I'll guess that it's a fluffy long-haired cat."

"I guess it's, um, a cute potbelly pig," Lolli said with a giggle.

"And the answer is…" Janey moved her

hand and looked.

Then she gasped. The picture wasn't of a cat, or of a potbelly pig, either. It wasn't anything cute at all.

It showed a cowering, matted, skinny little gray dog chained in a bare yard.

5

Search and Rescue

"Oh, it's horrible!" Janey blurted out. She wished she hadn't seen the photo at all. The dog looked miserable. He had floppy ears and big, brown eyes. Other than that, he was so dirty and dusty that Janey couldn't even guess what kind of dog he was.

Lolli's eyes filled with tears. "Who would treat a dog like that?" she cried. "We have to do something!"

"What can we do?" Janey rubbed Roscoe's head.

"Let's go ask Mom and Dad." Lolli grabbed the tablet and hurried into the house.

The inside of the farmhouse smelled like scented candles, coffee, and Roscoe. Lolli's parents were sitting at the big wooden kitchen table drinking coffee and reading the Sunday newspaper.

When Lolli showed them the picture,

her mother looked concerned. "Oh, the poor thing," she said.

Lolli's father ran a hand through his curly hair. "Where did this photo come from, girls?" he asked.

"I'm not sure." Janey shrugged. "Whoever sent it didn't put her name on it."

"What can we do to help that dog?" Lolli asked her parents.

Mr. and Mrs. Simpson glanced at each other. "That's our girl," Mr. Simpson said. "'The only thing necessary for evil to triumph is for good men to do nothing.'"

"Huh?" Janey blinked. Was Lolli's dad going crazy, or did he think she and Lolli were men?

"It's a famous quotation," Mrs. Simpson explained with a smile. "It means we're very proud of you two for wanting to get involved."

Lolli's father nodded. "Why don't you forward that photo to the animal shelter?" he suggested. "The people there will know how to get the authorities on the case."

"Good idea." Janey found the shelter's website. She forwarded the photo of the skinny dog to the e-mail address on the contact page.

"I hope they can help that dog," Lolli said softly, staring at the photo.

Janey glanced at it one more time, then shuddered and clicked it off. She didn't want to look at the poor little dog's sad face any longer.

"Let's look at some nicer pictures now," she said.

But it didn't work. Janey couldn't stop thinking about the sad gray dog for the rest of the day.

· · · · · · · · · ·

"I can't stand it any longer," Janey told Lolli the next day at recess. "I'm going to ask Ms. Tanaka if I can call the shelter."

"Good idea," Lolli agreed.

Their homeroom teacher, Ms. Tanaka, was the playground monitor that day. Janey was glad it was her and not grumpy old Mr. Wells. Ms. Tanaka was young and wore cool clothes and laughed a lot.

"Oh, wow," Ms. Tanaka said when she heard about the neglected dog. "Go ahead and check in with the shelter. Here—you can use my phone."

"Thanks." Janey took the phone the

teacher handed her.

"Third Street Animal Shelter, may I help you?" a familiar-sounding voice answered when Janey called the shelter's number.

"Kitty? Is that you?" Janey said. She told the shelter worker who she was and why she was calling.

"Oh, I'm so glad you checked in, Janey," Kitty replied. "Do you know anything else about the dog in that photo?"

"No." Janey clutched the phone tighter. "That's why I sent it to you guys. That dog needs help!"

"Oh, yes, we agree." Kitty sounded apologetic. "We forwarded the photo to the town's animal control officer. But she can't take action since nobody knows where the dog is located. If you can find out more, please call us back, okay?"

"Um, okay." Janey wasn't sure how Kitty expected her to find out more. She was just a kid!

She hung up the phone and gave it back to Ms. Tanaka. The teacher was listening to a third grader complain about a boy teasing her, so she just nodded and smiled.

Then Janey went back over to Lolli and told her what Kitty had said. "Now what?" Janey finished. "We have to figure out how to help that dog!"

"Yes, definitely," Lolli agreed, looking worried. She glanced toward the playing field, where several kids were kicking a soccer ball around. "Adam's over there. Let's see if he has any ideas."

They called Adam over, showed him the

dog's picture, and told him what was going on. "Wow," he said with a frown. "That's messed up. How can anyone keep a dog that way?"

"Have you ever seen this dog?" Janey asked him. "You know—while you're out walking dogs and stuff?"

"No way." Adam shook his head. "I'd definitely remember!"

Janey bit her lip. Adam walked dogs all over town. "What if that dog isn't even around here?" she wondered. "It could come from a town miles away. Then we'll never find—hey, watch it!"

Zach was zooming straight toward her on his skateboard. He stopped just in time to avoid crashing into her.

"Hey." He grinned. "I didn't scare you, did I? So how's the blog business?"

Janey didn't answer. She wished Zach would go away. But Lolli and Adam started telling him about the skinny dog.

"...but we don't know where the dog is, so they can't help him," Lolli finished.

"No problem." Zach grabbed Janey's

tablet out of her hand. "I can find out who sent the photo. Then all you have to do is track him down and ask where he saw the dog."

"You can?" Adam brightened. "How?"

Zach was already typing on the keypad. "You need to have a verified name and address to post on the blog," he mumbled as he worked. "It's part of the kid-safe software." He hit one more key. "Here you go—this is who sent that picture."

"Vanessa Chaudhry," Lolli read aloud. Her eyes widened. "Hey, she goes to this school!"

Janey knew Vanessa, too. She was the best singer in the fifth grade—she always had solos in the school concerts. "The fifth graders should be coming out for recess while we're on our way in," Janey said. "Let's try to talk to her then."

Vanessa looked startled when Janey and the others surrounded her a few minutes later. At first she tried to deny she'd taken the picture. But when Janey told her that the animal shelter couldn't help the dog without more information, Vanessa bit her lip.

"Oh! I thought posting the picture would be enough," she said. "I really want someone to rescue that poor dog."

"Then tell us where he is!" Janey urged. "We won't tell anyone you told us."

"Okay." Vanessa described where she'd seen the dog. It was a rural area on the opposite side of town from Lolli's farm. "I really hope you can help him," Vanessa added as Ms. Tanaka headed over to shoo

Janey and her classmates inside. "No dog should have to live like that."

6

Truman Is Safe!

"They got him!" Janey cried, bursting out of the school's main office.

It was the next afternoon. Mr. Wells had dismissed the class a few minutes earlier. Janey had run straight to the office so she could use the phone there to call the shelter.

"Hip hip hooray!" Lolli cheered, jumping up and down. "What did Kitty say?"

"The animal control officer went out yesterday and talked to the dog's owners," Janey said. She and Lolli wandered down the hall toward the school exit. "They agreed to give the dog to the shelter. He's there now!"

"We should go see him!" Lolli grabbed Janey's arm. "Let's call home and see if our parents will let us walk over to the shelter."

They turned around and rushed back to the office. They got there at the same time as Ms. Tanaka.

"Everything okay, girls?" the teacher asked.

"Yes," Janey replied. "We just need to use the phone."

Ms. Tanaka nodded and held the door open for them. Then the teacher went to check her office mail cubby as the girls headed toward the desk to ask the secretary for permission to use the phone.

"You can call first," Janey told Lolli.

Lolli's father gave permission right away.

But when Janey called home, her mother sounded reluctant. "Maybe you should come home first," she said. "I can drive you and Lolli to the shelter."

"Please, Mom. We don't want to wait that long. Besides, the shelter is only a few blocks from school," Janey said. "Lolli's parents already said yes."

"That's right, Mrs. Whitfield," Lolli said,

leaning over Janey's shoulder to talk into the phone. "We'll be careful, we promise!"

"Did I hear you girls say you're going to the Third Street Shelter?" Ms. Tanaka asked, walking over.

"Maybe," Janey said. "If I can talk my mom into saying yes."

Ms. Tanaka smiled. "If it helps, you can tell her I'll walk there with you," she offered. "I was thinking about heading over there myself."

Her offer did help. Janey's mother finally said it was okay. Soon Janey, Lolli, and Ms. Tanaka were walking down the sidewalk toward Third Street.

"Why are you going to the shelter?" Lolli asked her teacher.

Ms. Tanaka chuckled. "Actually, you

guys inspired me. I just moved to a new apartment last month, and this one allows pets. I've been thinking about getting a dog, and hearing you talk about the shelter made me decide it's time to start looking for the perfect best friend."

"That's awesome!" For a second, Janey was envious. It seemed everyone could have a pet except her! Then she had a great idea. "I know—you should adopt the dog we saved!"

"Hmm. I like the idea of rescuing a dog that really needs me." Ms. Tanaka sounded interested. "What does he look like?"

Janey showed her the picture from her blog. "He looks kind of bad here," she said. "But I bet all he needs is a good brushing and some food and he'll be supercute!"

"Oh, he's cute—but awfully small. I was thinking about a bigger dog." Ms. Tanaka smiled. "See, I had horses growing up, so I'm used to big pets. A really huge dog is the next best thing to a horse!"

Lolli laughed, while Janey smiled weakly. "Are you sure you don't want him?" she asked.

"Sorry." Ms. Tanaka patted her arm. "But don't worry—your dog is adorable. I'm sure he'll find a home fast."

When they reached the shelter, Ms. Tanaka said good-bye and headed into the dog room. Meanwhile, Kitty rushed over to greet the girls.

"I'm so glad you came!" she said. "Stay right here, and I'll go get Truman so he can thank you in person!"

"Truman?" Janey echoed.

"That's the dog you saved. He's a real sweetie." Kitty smiled. "Be right back."

Moments later she returned with a dog on a leash. Janey barely recognized him from his picture! Someone had given him a bath, brushed the tangles out of his silky fur, and trimmed the hair on his ears and paws.

Janey had memorized every breed from her dog books, and she thought Truman looked as if he might be a cross between a schnauzer and a shih tzu. Whatever he was, he was one of the cutest dogs she'd ever seen!

"Oh, you're so adorable!" she cried, reaching for him.

Truman ducked away from her touch, but he wagged his short tail and pricked up his ears with curiosity. "You'll have to take it easy and be patient with him," Kitty advised. "He's still a little shy. But he's very sweet once he trusts you. Come on—let's hang out in the Meet and Greet room so you can all get to know each other."

They all went into the small room. Truman sniffed everything carefully, then flopped down on one of the beanbag chairs.

Meanwhile Kitty told the girls what the animal officer had found out.

"Truman belonged to an elderly man who adored him," she said. "Then the owner died and Truman went to live with the man's relatives. But one of the kids in the house was allergic."

"Just like Janey's dad," Lolli said.

Janey nodded. "The family stuck him outside and kind of forgot about him, I guess. One of the other kids was supposed to feed him and give him water but he didn't always remember."

Janey clenched her fists. "How could anyone be so horrible?" she exclaimed. "Especially with a sweet dog like Truman!"

"Try not to think about it," Lolli advised. "He's safe now, and I'm sure somebody great will adopt him."

"I wish I could adopt him," Janey said.

Lolli gave her a sympathetic smile. "Try not to think about that, either."

Janey tried. For the next hour, she and Lolli stayed with Truman. He was shy at first, but eventually he seemed to decide the girls were okay. After that, they could hardly get him to stop playing!

Janey was disappointed when her mother arrived to pick them up. "We'll come visit you again soon, Truman," she promised the little dog.

"Right," Lolli agreed. "Unless someone adopts you before that!"

"I'm sure it won't take long." Janey smiled and rubbed Truman's silky ears. She giggled as the little dog licked her from her chin to her forehead. "Who could resist a face—or a tongue—like that?"

7

Still Waiting

"Did you call the shelter last night?" Lolli asked when Janey walked into school on Thursday morning.

Janey nodded and sighed. "He's still there."

"I don't get it." Lolli leaned against the wall of cubbies, watching as Janey put her stuff away. "Truman is such a great dog! Why doesn't anyone want to take him home?"

"I have no idea." Janey was about to put her tablet in the cubby with the rest of her things. Then she stopped and stared at it.

"But I just thought of something. My blog was what saved Truman, right? Maybe it can also help him find the perfect home!"

"What do you mean?" Lolli asked.

Janey was already logging on to the Internet. "I'm going to post an update about Truman. Lots of people saw the picture of him on my blog."

"That's true," Lolli agreed. "You got tons of comments about how horrible he looked."

"So now I'll tell everyone he's safe and looking for a home." Janey typed quickly, describing how the animal officer had saved Truman. She added that the little dog was at the shelter waiting for an adopter to come and take him home.

Lolli watched over her shoulder. "Don't forget to mention how cute he looks now that he's healthy and clean," she suggested.

Janey nodded. She wished she'd taken pictures of Truman at the shelter. Maybe she could get some later. But her words would have to do for now.

"There!" she said, hitting the key to post the blurb. "That should do the trick."

· · · · · · · · · ·

But when Janey called the shelter again on Saturday, Kitty told her that Truman was still there.

"Your ad *did* work, though," Kitty added. "Sort of, anyway. Three different people came in looking for Truman because they'd seen him on your blog."

"Really? Then why is he still there?" Janey asked.

"They all decided he wasn't quite

right for them," Kitty said. "They all chose different dogs instead."

"Oh." Janey sighed. "Oh, well, lots of people come to get new pets on the weekend, right? Someone will probably take him home soon. Lolli and I will be right over—we want to see him again before he finds his new owners."

Soon the two friends were at the shelter playing with Truman. A family was in the Meet and Greet room getting to know a few of the shelter's cats, so the girls tossed a rubber bone for Truman in the wide, rubber-paved aisle of the dog room. There were dogs in the runs on either side of the aisle, but Truman paid little attention to them, staying focused on the girls.

"Good boy!" Janey exclaimed when

Truman pounced on the bone and then brought it back to her. "You already know how to fetch!"

"He's supersmart." said Lolli as she ruffled Truman's ears. "Aren't you, boy?"

Just then the door to the dog room opened. Kitty walked in, followed by a nicely dressed man and woman and a five-year-old boy.

"Excuse me, girls," Kitty said. "This lovely family has come to see Truman."

"That's right." The mother had a nice smile. "Are you Janey? We saw what you wrote about Truman on your blog, and we just had to meet him!"

Her husband nodded. "We were planning to get a dog this weekend anyway, and we think Truman might be perfect. Is that him?"

"Yes, this is Truman." Janey saw that Truman was backing away from the man. "Um, he's a little shy with new people."

"He's cute! Here, Truman!" The little boy rushed toward Truman, who quickly sidled out of reach.

"Slow down, son," his father called. "You don't want to startle him."

He strode over and grabbed Truman before the little dog could get away. "Careful," Kitty warned. "He's still getting used to things here, and…"

"Easy, fella! We just want to pet you, that's all." The man hugged Truman to his chest. Truman struggled against his grip, looking anxious.

"Why don't you let me hold him for you?" Janey said quickly. "He knows me, so that will help him relax."

"Ow!" the man said as Truman scrabbled against his chest, looking frantic now. "Oh, no! He just put a hole in my new shirt!"

He set Truman down and peered down at his golf shirt. Truman darted behind Janey and pressed himself against her legs. She could feel him trembling.

"It's just a shirt, Steve," the man's wife said, rolling her eyes. "But perhaps Truman isn't quite right for us after all. We don't want a dog we need to tiptoe around."

The little boy already seemed to have forgotten all about Truman. He was over by one of the runs, reaching in to pet a friendly hound mix.

"I want this one!" he cried. "Look—he likes me!"

"Can we meet that one?" the man asked Kitty. "He seems like a good family dog."

Kitty shot Truman an anxious glance. "Sure, let's take him over to the Meet and Greet," she said. "I think the cats are out of there now."

As soon as the family had disappeared, along with Kitty and the hound mix, Truman came out of hiding. He grabbed the rubber bone and dropped it at Lolli's feet, wagging his tail.

Janey sighed. "Oh, Truman," she said, kneeling down to give the dog a hug. "You're such a sweetie pie. Why can't anyone but us see that?"

8

A Plan for Truman

A little while later, Kitty returned. "Well, at least Chance found a new home," she said, gesturing at the empty run where the hound mix had been. "That family loved him, and it was totally mutual. I think it's a great match." She bent to pat Truman, who was sniffing at her shoe. "I just wish this little guy would find his perfect match."

"Me, too," Janey said. "I can't believe nobody wants him!"

Kitty sighed. "I know. Poor Truman was just a little too shy or a little too untrained for all the people who were interested in him so far."

Just then the door opened again. Zach burst into the dog room, followed by his mother. "Yo, Truman!" Zach exclaimed loudly when he spotted the dog. "Are these girls bothering you, little guy?"

He rushed over to the dog. Janey expected Truman to try to get away, but instead he barked and jumped up on Zach's legs. Zach laughed and rubbed Truman's ears.

"Hey, he's being friendly now," Lolli said.

"Sure he is, he's my buddy." Zach grabbed the rubber bone and tossed it. Truman barked and leaped off to retrieve it.

Dr. Goldman chuckled. "Don't even think about asking again to take him home," she warned Zach. She glanced at the girls. "Zach was with me when I did Truman's intake checkup and shots the other day. As you can see, the two of them hit it off."

"Is that why you two stopped by?" Kitty asked the vet with a grin. "To adopt Truman?"

"Actually, I stopped by to take that new cat's stitches out. Seeing Truman is a bonus, but I'm afraid we can't take him home. We already have a cat, which is about all I can handle with four boys, a busy vet practice, and an absentminded husband who gets so caught up in his work that he's not likely to remember to walk a dog unless it's actually piddling on his foot." She smiled at Janey and Lolli. "Is one of you thinking about adopting Truman?"

"Our parents won't let us take him home, either," Janey said. "And nobody else seems interested, even though he's so fab!"

"Poor Truman." Lolli patted Truman as he trotted past with the rubber bone. "He just needs someone who understands him."

"Maybe." Dr. Goldman pushed Truman down gently as he dropped the bone, barked, and jumped up on her legs. "But he could also use a little training and socializing to make him more adoptable."

"What do you mean?" Janey asked.

"He's a nice dog," the vet said. "But some adopters might not be able to see the diamond in the rough the way we can." She smiled at Janey and Lolli. "If you girls want to help him find a home, maybe you can work with him a little. Teach him a few basic commands, and get him more used to being around people."

"We can do that!" Janey felt a surge of hope. "Right, Lolli?"

"Definitely!" Lolli agreed.

"Yeah," Zach put in. "I can help if you want."

"Thanks, but that's okay," Janey told him. "We've got it covered. Come on Lolli, let's start right now!"

Kitty smiled apologetically. "Actually, you'll need to get your parents to sign our volunteer form before you can do any real training or take him for walks outside," she said. "Sorry. I probably shouldn't even have let you spend all this time with him before doing that."

Janey frowned, feeling impatient. But Lolli nodded. "We can do that," she said. "We were planning to ask about volunteering here anyway, and both our parents already said it was okay, so I'm sure they'll sign. I'll call my mom to come get us, and then we'll be back as soon as we have the forms filled out and signed."

"You girls are lucky that this shelter lets kids volunteer," Dr. Goldman told them with a smile. "I would've loved to get involved like that as a kid, but the shelter in the town where I grew up only allows people over eighteen to handle the animals."

"Not here," Kitty said cheerfully. "We've found that younger kids are great with the animals! Come on, girls—let's get you those forms."

. . . .

Over the next week, Janey went to the shelter as often as she could to work with

Truman. Lolli usually came, too. Even Adam took some time out of his busy dog-walking schedule to show the girls some training techniques. Janey knew that Adam had worked with lots of dogs, but she was impressed by how quickly he taught Truman

the commands for sit, stay, come, and heel.

Truman seemed to enjoy all the attention. After a few days, Kitty reported that he was already acting friendlier with people—even ones he didn't know.

"He's a fast learner," she said as she watched Truman follow Janey around the lobby on Friday afternoon, staying right at her heel. "And you kids are great teachers! I bet he'll find his new family before long."

"I sure hope you're right. Sit, Truman!" Janey beamed as the little dog lowered his haunches to the floor. "Good boy!"

9

A Perfect Pair?

"I wish we didn't have to take him back to the shelter," Janey said as she turned the corner onto Third Street. It was early Sunday afternoon and she, Lolli, and Adam had just helped Kitty take Truman to the town park for a walk. The little dog had behaved perfectly, walking politely on his leash, letting several strangers pet him, and even standing quietly while a woman pushed a screaming baby past in a stroller.

"We shouldn't keep him out too long, though," Adam pointed out. "Lots of people come to the shelter on Sundays."

"That's right." Kitty gave a gentle tug on Truman's leash as he stopped to sniff at a leaf on the sidewalk. "We don't want him to miss being seen by his perfect adopter."

"True." Janey felt a pang of sadness. Even though they were all working hard to make Truman more adoptable, she hated to think that she might not get to see him anymore once he went to his new home.

When they entered the lobby, Truman barked and leaped forward. Zach and his mother were by the desk with one of Kitty's coworkers. Zach was balanced on one foot on his skateboard while Dr. Goldman examined a fat white cat's paw.

"Hi, Truman!" Zach exclaimed, hurrying forward to greet the little dog. "What's up?"

"We just went for a walk." Janey took Truman's leash from Kitty, and pulled him in closer. "Truman did fab. We're still working on his training, you know."

"Yeah, I heard." Zach rubbed Truman's head. "I bet someone will adopt him soon."

Janey nodded, stepping out of the way as the other shelter worker walked past carrying the white cat. "I'm thinking of posting again on my blog about how great Truman is doing," Janey said. "I bet that will get more people to come see him."

The bell over the shelter door tinkled as someone entered. Janey was surprised to see that it was Ms. Tanaka.

"Hi, kids!" The teacher seemed surprised to see them, too. She smiled. "You sure spend a lot of time here, don't you?"

"What can I say?" Zach shrugged and hooked a thumb toward his mother. "My mom drags me here all the time."

"I think she was talking to us," Janey informed him. "Hi, Ms. T. Didn't you already pick out a dog last weekend?" She'd been so busy thinking about Truman that she'd almost forgotten about her teacher's quest for a pet. But now she was curious.

"Not yet." The teacher shrugged. "There are lots of great dogs here, but I couldn't decide on one, so I decided to wait and think about it."

"So you came back for another look?" Kitty asked cheerfully. "I can help you as soon as I finish showing Dr. Goldman her next patient, okay?"

"No hurry, thanks." Ms. Tanaka smiled as Kitty and Dr. Goldman headed off into the dog room. Then she patted Truman as he trotted over to say hi. "Who have we here?"

"This is Truman—the dog we showed you before," Lolli told her.

Ms. Tanaka looked surprised. "Really? Wow, I didn't recognize him! He looks totally different from that poor, scraggly dog in the picture." She rubbed his ears, smiling as he slurped her hands and then rolled onto his back, begging for a belly rub. "Too bad he's not a little bigger."

Janey shot Lolli and Adam a look. Ms. Tanaka really seemed to like Truman—and he seemed to like her, too. Maybe they'd given up on her too easily!

"He might not be that big, but he's got a huge personality," Janey told Ms. Tanaka. "He's just about fully trained, too—watch!" She snapped her fingers to get Truman's attention. "Truman, heel!"

She quickly put Truman through his paces, demonstrating all the commands he could do. Truman got a little distracted when a shelter worker led a tiny, fluffy dog past, heading for the Meet and Greet room. But otherwise he was practically perfect!

When the demonstration was finished, Ms. Tanaka was smiling. "Very impressive, Janey," she said. "Truman is cute. He'll make someone a fantastic friend. I'm just not sure he's quite what I'm looking for."

"Are you sure?" Janey's heart sank. What more could they do to convince her?

Zach stepped forward. "Can I take him for a sec?" he asked, reaching for Truman's leash.

Janey almost didn't hand him the leash. This was no time for Zach to start goofing around! She was sure if she could just figure out how to change Ms. Tanaka's mind somehow...

But she didn't resist as Zach took the leash. "Okay, Janey already showed you the boring stuff," he told Ms. Tanaka with a grin. "Now watch this!"

"What's he doing?" Lolli murmured, leaning toward Janey.

Janey shrugged. She watched as Zach kneeled down in front of Truman.

"Okay, Truman," he said, lifting his hand. "High-five!"

Truman barked. Then he jumped up, smacking his front paws onto Zach's palm.

"Oh, that's cute!" Ms. Tanaka exclaimed with a laugh. "Did you really teach him to high-five, Zach?"

"That's nothing," Zach said. "Check this out." He grabbed his skateboard and set it in front of Truman.

"Who taught Truman to high-five?" Lolli sounded confused.

Janey knew how she felt. She watched as Truman jumped onto Zach's skateboard and then used his hind leg to push off, barking happily as he rode the skateboard halfway across the lobby.

This time Ms. Tanaka laughed out loud and clapped. "That's so cool!" she exclaimed. "Did you teach him that, Zach? Very

impressive!"

Zach grinned and bowed. "Thank you, it was nothing," he said. "I've been coming by and teaching Truman a few tricks while Mom's here working."

Janey frowned, not sure whether to be impressed or annoyed. Then she noticed that Ms. Tanaka was kneeling down and patting Truman, whose whole body seemed to be wagging as he enjoyed the attention.

"Truman is great, isn't he?" Janey told her teacher. And then she had an idea. "He's kind of like a big dog in a little dog's body, right?"

"Yeah," Adam put in. "I've worked with a lot of dogs, and Truman is one of the coolest. Seriously."

Lolli nodded vigorously. "And I think he really likes you, Ms. Tanaka."

The teacher laughed, holding up her hands. "Okay, enough with the hard sell, gang," she said. "You don't need to convince me—Truman already did that."

"What? Really?" Janey wasn't sure she'd heard her right.

"Really." Ms. Tanaka gave Truman one last pat, then straightened up. "Actually, I've been thinking my apartment might be kind of small for a big dog. And now I'm totally convinced. Besides, a bigger dog couldn't ride a skateboard like that, right?" She winked. "Anyway, when Kitty comes back I think I'll talk to her about taking Truman home with me so I can see what other fun tricks I can teach him. What do you say, Truman?"

Truman barked and danced around her legs. Janey let out a whoop of joy. Talk about a happy ending!

10

Happy Endings...
and Beginnings

"Leave that alone, Roscoe." Lolli tugged on her dog's leash as he stopped to sniff at a pinecone on the sidewalk. "Come on, we're almost there."

Janey stopped to let them catch up. It was Tuesday afternoon, and she and Lolli had decided to take Roscoe to the town park.

"Hey, look who's here!" Lolli said as they entered the park. "It's Ms. Tanaka and Truman!"

Janey looked where she was pointing.

Their teacher was halfway across the park in a grassy area shaded by some huge old oak trees. Truman was there, too, chasing a ball his new owner was throwing for him.

"I still can't believe how great everything turned out." Lolli smiled as she watched the pair playing. "It's like it was meant to be!"

"I know, right?" Janey nodded. "Ms. Tanaka told me she can't imagine her life without Truman. Isn't that fab?"

"Totally fab," Lolli agreed. "Should we go over and say hi?"

Before she could answer, Janey heard a flurry of barking from the opposite direction. Turning to look, she saw Adam coming with one of his doggy clients, a pretty collie mix. Zach was with him, pushing himself along on his skateboard.

Roscoe's whole hind end wagged along with his tail as he greeted the other dog. The collie mix barked, then came forward to sniff Roscoe's nose.

"It's okay," Adam told Lolli. "This guy is

friendly with other dogs. And I know Roscoe is, too."

Zach was peering across the park. "Hey, there's Ms. T. and Truman," he said.

"Yeah, we just saw them, too," Janey said. "We were about to go say hi. Want to come?"

"In a minute." Adam glanced at Zach. "Actually, it's good that we ran into you. Zach has an idea he wants to tell you about."

"An idea?" Janey looked at Zach. "What kind of idea?"

Zach flipped his skateboard and tried to jump back on, but he missed and staggered off a few steps. "It's an idea about breaking my leg," he joked. "I'm working on it now."

Adam smiled. "No, seriously, tell them, dude," he said. "I think they'll like it."

"What is it, Zach?" Lolli asked.

Zach patted Roscoe as the big dog came over to sniff at him. "It's no big deal," he said. "Just something I was thinking about, you know? After what happened with Truman, and everything...."

Janey sighed. "Just spit it out already," she said. "We don't have all day."

Zach smirked. "Why not? Do you have an appointment with the President of the United States or something?"

"Just tell them," Adam said.

Zach shrugged. "Okay. See, we did such a great job getting Truman the perfect home, right? All of us helped."

"That's true," Lolli agreed.

Janey nodded. She had to admit that Zach's tricks had probably won over Ms.

Tanaka just as much as the training she, Lolli, and Adam had done.

"So." Zach paused, glancing over toward Truman again. "I was thinking we should, you know, do more of that."

"You mean we should volunteer at the shelter?" Janey said. "We're already planning to."

"Not just that," Adam said. "He thinks we should form, like, a club or something."

"Yeah." Zach sounded excited now. "I was thinking we could call it the Pet Rescue Club! I bet there are lots of other animals right here in our town who need our help. We could use your blog to find them, and then to help find them homes— just like with Truman. And, well, like I said the four of us make a pretty good team..."

Lolli smiled. "What a super idea!" she exclaimed.

But Janey hesitated. She wasn't so sure. For one thing, Zach was pretty annoying sometimes. Did she really want to be in a club with him?

"What do you think, Janey?" Adam asked.

"I don't know," Janey said slowly. "My blog is supposed to be for sharing cute pet photos, not for stuff like that. Seeing that first picture of Truman pop up was really upsetting."

"I know, but it could be for both things, couldn't it?" Lolli said, stroking the collie mix's sleek head. "We'll be able to help other dogs like Truman. And cats and other animals, too, of course."

"Isn't that worth being upset a little bit?" Adam added.

Zach didn't say anything. He was watching Janey carefully, not cracking jokes or messing with his skateboard for once. Janey stared back at him. Would he really take something like this seriously?

She wasn't sure, but she realized something else. It didn't matter. She took helping animals seriously. So did Lolli and Adam, and probably Zach. Working together, she was sure they could make it work.

"I guess you're right," she said with a cautious smile. "Helping Truman made it all worthwhile. And my blog has been getting tons of hits. Everyone loved hearing about Truman's happy ending. It really is the perfect way to reach animals in need."

"Cool!" Zach exclaimed with a grin. "So we're going to do this?"

He raised his hand. Lolli high-fived him. Adam switched the leash he was holding to his other hand and did the same. Then Janey stepped forward and high-fived Zach, too. At least she tried to—at the last second, he pulled his hand away.

"Psych!" he cried with a grin.

Janey frowned. "Very funny."

"Sorry." Zach grabbed her hand and high-fived it. "So it's official—we're the Pet Rescue Club?"

"Yeah." Janey's mind was already filling with ideas for how to make the club work. It was going to be great! She couldn't believe she hadn't thought of it herself. "It's official. I can't wait to get started!"

Meet the
Real Truman!

A little gray dog named Harry Truman was surrendered to a shelter in Tennessee in 2010. He was skinny and had matted fur. He was sent to a shelter in upstate New York, where he met his future owner. She considered herself a "big dog" person, but Harry Truman convinced her that even little dogs have big hearts!

No Time
for Hallie

For Queen Rags and Buddy, who let me
stray onto their property.

—C. H.

Bird Alert

"Good kitty, Mulberry." Janey Whitfield patted the fat orange tabby cat that had just jumped onto the sofa beside her. She giggled as he rubbed his face on her arm. "Your whiskers tickle! Aw, but that's okay— you love me, don't you?"

"He's just hoping you'll give him more food," Zach Goldman said with a laugh.

Mulberry was Zach's family's cat. Janey was at Zach's house, along with their friends Lolli Simpson and Adam Santos. Today was the first official meeting of the Pet

Rescue Club—the group the four of them had decided to form after helping to rescue a neglected dog named Truman.

The meeting had started half an hour earlier. Zach's dad had brought out some snacks, and the four kids were supposed to be discussing how to organize their new group. But they'd been too busy eating and playing with Mulberry to do much discussing so far.

Lolli selected a piece of cheese off the tray on the coffee table. "Did you add the stuff about the Pet Rescue Club to the blog?" she asked Janey.

"Yes." Janey pushed Mulberry away gently. Then she picked up her tablet computer and showed Lolli the screen.

Janey's blog had started as a way for kids around their town to share photos of their pets. Janey loved animals, but she couldn't have a pet of her own because her father was severely allergic to anything with fur or feathers. She'd thought that seeing pictures of lots of cute pets would be the next best thing to having her own.

Now the blog had another purpose, too.

The Pet Rescue Club was going to use it to find animals that needed their help. So far Janey had written an update on Truman and added a paragraph telling people to send in information on any animal that might need their help.

"Okay," Adam said. "So we put something on the blog. Now what?"

Adam was a very practical person. He was so responsible that he already had a successful pet-sitting business, even though he was only nine. People all over town paid him to come to their houses to feed and walk their dogs while they were at work or on vacation.

Janey didn't answer Adam right away. Mulberry was kneading his front paws on her leg and purring. Janey rubbed the cat's head and smiled.

"I wish I could have a cat like Mulberry," she said.

"Yeah, Mulberry is great!" Lolli leaned over to pet the cat. Mulberry turned around and butted his head against her arm.

Janey giggled. "And he's so cute! Here, Mulberry—want a cracker?"

"Don't give him that," Zach said quickly. "It's onion flavored and cats shouldn't eat onion—it's bad for them."

"Really?" Janey wasn't sure whether to believe him. Zach was always joking around and playing pranks on people. Still, she didn't want to hurt Mulberry if Zach was being serious for once. She pulled the cracker away and glanced at Adam. "Is that true? Are onions bad for cats?"

Adam shrugged. "Probably. I know dogs aren't supposed to eat onions."

"Why are you asking him? Don't you believe me?" Zach asked Janey. "My mom's a vet, you know. She's taught me lots of stuff like that."

Before Janey could answer, a pair of twelve-year-old boys raced into the room.

They were identical twins. Both of them were tall and skinny with wavy dark hair and the same brown eyes as Zach. It was raining outside, and the boys' sneakers left wet tracks on the floor.

Janey knew the twins were two of Zach's three older brothers. She couldn't imagine living with that many boys!

"Check it out," one of the twins said, pointing at Janey. "Little Zachie has a girlfriend!"

"No way—he has two girlfriends! Way to go, little bro!" the other boy exclaimed with a grin.

"Shut up!" Zach scowled at them. "And go away. We're trying to have a meeting here."

One of the twins stepped over and grabbed Mulberry off the sofa. "Yo, Mulberry," he said, cuddling the cat. "Are these girls bothering you?"

"Mulberry likes us," Lolli said with a smile. "He's like the mascot of the Pet Rescue

Club."

"Okay." The twin dropped Mulberry on the sofa again. The cat sat down and started washing his paw.

"Grab the umbrella and let's go," the other twin said. "The guys are waiting for us outside."

One of the twins grabbed an umbrella off a hook by the back door. Then they raced back out of the room.

"Sorry about that," Zach muttered. "They are so annoying."

"They're not so bad." Lolli smiled. She got along with everybody—even obnoxious boys. "Anyway, what were we talking about?"

"About how cats can't eat onion," Zach said. "They shouldn't have chocolate, either. Did you know that?" He stared at Janey.

She shrugged. "No. That's interesting."

"Yeah," Lolli agreed. "There's lots to know about having a pet! When we first got Roscoe, I thought all he needed was a bowl of water and some dog food. But there's a lot more to it than that!"

Roscoe was the Simpsons' big, lovable dog. Lolli and her parents had found him at the Third Street Shelter a few years earlier. He was a mix of Labrador retriever, rottweiler, and who knew what else.

"I have an idea," Janey said. "You already said Mulberry was our club mascot. We should make Roscoe a mascot, too. We can post their pictures on the blog to make it official."

"Good idea," Lolli said. "I have a cute picture of Roscoe we can use."

"We should take a picture of Mulberry riding on my skateboard," Zach said. "That would be cool!"

"Veto," Janey replied.

Zach frowned at her. "Can't you just say no like a normal person?" he asked. "Oh, wait, I forgot—you're not normal."

Janey ignored him. "Veto" was her new favorite word. Janey liked finding interesting words and using them. Saying veto was her new way of saying no.

"Hey Janey," Adam spoke up. "I think I heard your tablet ping."

"Really?" Janey had dropped her tablet on the sofa. Now Mulberry was sitting on it. She pulled the tablet out from under the cat. "Sorry, Mulberry. That might be an animal who needs our help!"

Lolli leaned over her shoulder. "What does it say?"

"It's not a posting on the blog," Janey said. "It's alerting me to a new e-mail."

She clicked into her e-mail account. The message was from a classmate named Leah. Janey read it quickly.

Hi Janey,

I heard you're helping animals now. I need help! I just got home from my soccer practice and found out my pet canary is missing!

2

Runaway Cat?

"Oh, no!" Janey exclaimed, reading the e-mail again.

"What's wrong?" Adam asked.

"The e-mail is from Leah," Janey said. "She says her canary is missing!"

"Leah has a canary?" Lolli said. "I didn't know that."

"I didn't either. But if it's missing, we should try to help her find it," Janey said. "Zach, can I use the phone?"

"Sure, that'll be five dollars, please," Zach said.

Janey ignored the joke. She rushed into the kitchen and grabbed the phone. Leah had put her number at the end of the e-mail.

"Janey?" Leah said from the other end of the line. "I was hoping you'd call. I'm so worried about Sunny!"

"What happened?" Janey asked.

"I must have forgotten to latch Sunny's cage after I fed him this morning before school." Leah sounded upset. "When I got home, the cage door was open and he was nowhere in sight!"

"Oh, no!" Janey exclaimed.

"That's not even the worst part," Leah went on. "My bedroom window was open! What if he flew outside? I might never find him!"

Janey glanced at Lolli, Adam, and Zach. They had followed her into the kitchen and were all listening to her half of the conversation.

"Don't worry, Leah," Janey said. "The Pet Rescue Club is on it! We'll be right over."

She hung up and told the others what Leah had said. "I don't like the idea of keeping birds cooped up in cages," Lolli said uncertainly. "Shouldn't they be free to fly around?"

"I don't know," Janey said. "But Leah sounded really worried."

"Then we should help her," Lolli said.

"Definitely," Zach agreed, and Adam nodded.

Mulberry had followed Janey into the kitchen, too. He rubbed against her legs. Then, suddenly, he meowed and rushed over to the screen door leading outside.

"Mulberry, what are you doing?" Lolli asked.

"Look!" Adam pointed. "There's another cat out there!"

Janey saw it, too. A cute black cat with big green eyes was looking in at them from outside!

"Where did that cat come from?" Lolli wondered.

"I don't know." Janey stepped closer and peered at the cat. "It's not wearing a collar or tags. But it looks healthy—just wet from the rain."

"I think I know where that cat lives," Zach said. "I've seen her in the window of a house across the street."

Lolli looked concerned. "Uh-oh. What if she slipped out when her owners weren't looking? They'll be worried sick."

Adam nodded. "We should take her home."

"Yeah." Zach grinned. "This is the perfect chance for the Pet Rescue Club to rescue another pet!"

Janey felt impatient. "Okay, but hurry," she said. "Leah is waiting, remember?"

Zach ran to tell his father where they were going. Then the kids all went outside. Zach had to nudge Mulberry away from the door to stop him from following them.

The black cat was just as friendly as Mulberry. She rubbed against Lolli's legs and purred.

"Good kitty," Lolli said. "Can I pick you up?"

The cat purred louder. "I think she's

saying yes," Janey said with a smile.

Lolli picked up the cat. "Which house is it?" she asked, squinting in the light rain.

"That one." Zach pointed to a white house with black shutters. "My parents have met the people who live here, but I don't know them at all. They only moved in last summer."

All four kids checked for traffic and then crossed the street. The cat stayed snuggled in Lolli's arms.

Janey led the way up the steps onto the front porch of the white house. There was no doorbell, but there was a brass knocker shaped like a seashell. Janey reached up and rapped the knocker two or three times.

They waited but there was no response. "Maybe they're not home," Adam said.

"Try knocking one more time," Lolli suggested.

"Here, let me do it. Janey knocks like a girl." Zach pushed past the others and knocked harder. "There. If they're home, they should hear that."

Janey rolled her eyes at Lolli. Lolli just smiled.

Finally, there was the sound of footsteps from inside. Then the door swung open. A young woman was standing there. She was wearing sweatpants, and her hair was in a messy ponytail. A chubby baby with rosy cheeks was balanced on one hip.

"Oh, hello, kids," the woman said. "What are you doing with Hall Cat?"

"Hall Cat?" Lolli giggled. "Is that really her name?"

The young woman smiled back, though she didn't look that happy. "Yes, that's her," she said. "Was she bothering you? Sometimes she's too friendly for her own good."

"No, she wasn't bothering us," Janey said. "We thought you might be looking for her, though. We found her outside." She smiled at the baby. He was staring at her with big, blue eyes.

"Yes, my husband let her out a little while ago." The young woman shifted the baby to her other hip. "Hall Cat is sweet, but ever since the baby came, she always seems to be underfoot." She wiped a spot of drool off the baby's chin. "I'm afraid I might trip over her and drop him."

"Oh." Janey looked at Hall Cat. The cat was still purring away in Lolli's arms, looking content and calm. "Um, maybe you didn't know, but being outside can be dangerous for a house cat. She could get hit by a car, or—"

"This is a quiet neighborhood," the young mother broke in. "Anyway, we had

to do something. What if she scratched the baby while she was trying to play with him? I can't take that chance."

She sounded so worried that Janey couldn't help feeling sorry for her. But Janey was worried about Hall Cat, too.

"Maybe you could keep the baby's door shut," she said. "Or—"

Just then the baby let out a loud gurgle. The young woman glanced at him.

"Thanks for being so concerned about Hall Cat, kids," she said. "But trust me, being outside is the best option we have right now. My husband and I don't want to take her to the shelter, so she'll just have to adjust."

"The shelter?" Zach sounded alarmed.

"But—" Janey began.

Suddenly the baby opened his mouth and started to wail. His mother winced, then hugged him to her, rocking him back and forth.

"Sorry, I really have to go," she said. "You can leave Hall Cat on the porch if you want—she seems to like it there. Bye now!"

Before Janey could come up with another way to change the woman's mind, the door swung shut.

3

Search and Rescue

"I still don't think we should have left Hall Cat outside," Zach said. It was a few minutes later, and the Pet Rescue Club was halfway to Leah's house. She only lived a few blocks away in the same neighborhood.

"I know." Janey shrugged. "But what else could we do? Break into her owners' house and sneak her back in?"

"We're supposed to be the Pet Rescue Club." Lolli kicked at a stone on the sidewalk. "We should try to figure out how to help Hall Cat."

"We will," Janey said. "Right after we help Leah find her bird."

She felt sorry for Hall Cat, too. But she was even more worried about Leah's canary.

Soon the Pet Rescue Club was ringing Leah's doorbell. Leah answered right away. She was a tall, skinny girl with freckles and glasses. Normally she was always smiling or laughing, but today she looked anxious and sad.

"Thanks for coming," she said. "Come in and I'll show you Sunny's cage."

Janey and the others went inside. Leah's four-year-old brother was sitting on the living room floor playing with a toy car. Two cats were watching him. One was a gray tabby, and the other was mostly white with brown and orange patches.

"Cute kitties," Lolli told Leah.

"Thanks." Leah barely glanced at the cats as she headed for the stairs. Janey guessed that she was too worried about Sunny to think about anything else.

The Pet Rescue Club followed Leah to her bedroom upstairs. The room was painted pale yellow with white trim. Along one wall was a bird cage. It was very tall, with several

perches, a mirror, and colorful hanging toys.

"Wow." Lolli sounded impressed as she stepped closer for a better look. "This is a really nice cage!"

"Thanks," Leah said with a sad sigh. "Sunny loves it—at least I thought he did."

"It's so big," Zach commented. "Is it really all for one little bird?"

"Yes." Leah touched the cage. "Canaries need lots of room to fly. That's why Sunny's cage is so big."

"Really? That's interesting." Janey read everything she could about animals. But she didn't know that much about pet birds. "So you don't have any other canaries to keep Sunny company? Do you think that's why he flew away?"

Lolli nodded. "That makes sense. Maybe

he was looking for a friend."

"Dogs like having other dogs around," Adam agreed.

"Actually, male canaries do better living alone," Leah said. "And like I said, Sunny seemed really happy. I don't know why he'd try to escape!"

"We should try to find him." Adam walked over to the window and looked out. "Maybe he's still in your backyard."

All five of them hurried downstairs and out the back door. For the next half hour, they searched Leah's backyard. The yard was pretty big, and had lots of shrubs and flowers. Janey didn't like getting her hands dirty, but she was willing to do it to help an animal. She pulled back the branches of a prickly rose bush, looking for a flash of yellow. But there was no sign of Sunny.

"Here, birdie, birdie!" Zach called. He whistled loudly.

"Not like that," Leah corrected. "He likes it when I whistle to him like this."

She let out a soft, musical whistle. Janey tried to imitate it, and couldn't do it. But Adam imitated the whistle perfectly!

"Dude!" Zach said with a laugh. "You sound like a canary! I always knew you were a birdbrain!"

"Quit joking around," Janey told him. "We need to find Sunny before it gets dark."

"I know." Zach shot a look at Leah. "Sorry. I'll look over there behind the shed."

Another twenty minutes passed with no sign of Sunny. Finally, the back door opened and Leah's mom looked out.

"Leah, are you out there?" she called. "Sorry, but it's time for your friends to go home now. You need to set the table for dinner."

"But we haven't found Sunny yet!" Leah sounded frantic.

"I'm sorry, honey." Her mother did sound sorry, but she also sounded firm. "Maybe Sunny will find his way home on his own. There's nothing else you can do right now."

Leah sighed as her mother disappeared. "I'm so worried," she told Janey and the others, her voice quavering. "Poor little Sunny! He's not used to being out on his own."

"I know." Janey put an arm around her shoulders. "Try not to worry. The Pet Rescue

Club will figure something out. I promise."

··········

Zach hated waking up early. He always felt sleepy until almost lunchtime.

But the next morning when he looked out his bedroom window, he felt wide-awake right away. A small black shape was sitting on the sidewalk in front of his house.

"Hall Cat," Zach murmured. He tapped on the glass, but Hall Cat didn't hear him. She was watching a bird pecking at the grass nearby.

Moments later, Zach was dressed and heading for the door. He almost tripped over Mulberry, who was sleeping on the kitchen floor.

"Where are you going, dork?" his oldest brother, Josh, called out.

"Back in a sec," Zach said without slowing down.

Hall Cat came running when she saw Zach. She purred as he picked her up. Her fur felt soft and warm.

"Good girl," Zach whispered, tickling her chin. "I'm going to take you home, okay?"

Hall Cat kept purring. Zach carried her across the street. Even before he knocked on the door, he could hear the baby crying inside. A young man with a goatee answered

Zach's knock.

"Hi," Zach said. "I found your cat outside."

The man peered at him. "You're one of the boys from across the street, right?" he said. "Hi there. Oh, and don't worry about Hall Cat. She likes it outside."

"Maybe," Zach said. "But it's dangerous out there. Um, you know, cars and stuff." He tried to remember what else he'd heard Janey and the others say.

"No, it's cool, seriously." The man said smiling, but he looked distracted. "We've been putting her out whenever the baby's awake, and she's been fine."

Zach squeezed Hall Cat a little tighter, making her wiggle. He didn't want the man to close the door and leave Hall Cat outside. But Zach wasn't sure what to say to stop him.

He wished Janey was there—she always had lots of things to say. Or Adam, who knew so much about taking care of animals. Or Lolli—people seemed to like talking to her, even grownups.

"Um, how long have you had Hall Cat?" Zach blurted out.

The man glanced over his shoulder as another loud wail came from somewhere inside. "Quite a while," he said. He chuckled. "Longer than I've had my wife, actually."

"Really?" Zach said.

The man reached out to scratch Hall Cat under the chin, which made her purr even louder. "I got her in college actually," he said. "I was living in a fraternity house and found her huddled under the front porch. She was super-friendly, but none of our neighbors knew where she came from. So we kept her." He smiled. "She sort of became our fraternity mascot and visited everyone who lived on my hall. That's why we called her Hall Cat. After I graduated she stayed with me and the name had stuck."

"That's pretty funny," Zach said with a grin.

The man grinned back. "Anyway, when I got married a few years later, Hall Cat came to live with us. My wife had never had a pet before, but she's always liked Hall Cat." He sighed and glanced over his shoulder again as the baby let out a loud squawk somewhere inside. "But now, with the new baby, she's just a little overwhelmed and worried about what might happen, you know?"

Zach didn't really know what the man meant by that. Before he could ask, he heard a loud wheezing and clanking sound from the far end of the block.

"Oops," he said. "That's the school bus. Gotta go!"

He leaned to one side, tossing Hall Cat gently past the man into the house. "Hey!" the man exclaimed, sounding surprised.

But Zach didn't stick around to find out whether the man threw Hall Cat back out or let her stay in. His backpack was still at home, and he'd have to run if he wanted to grab it before the bus got there.

4
Questions and Answers

When Janey got to school, she headed to Leah's cubby before even visiting her own. Leah was there putting her books away.

"Did you find him?" Janey asked. As soon as Leah turned around, Janey could guess the answer. Leah still looked sad and worried.

"No," Leah said with a loud sigh. "I got up early this morning to search in the yard some more, but all I saw out there were wild birds and a few squirrels."

"Oh." Janey chewed her lower lip. "Okay,

try not to worry. I'll figure something out, I promise."

She found Lolli at her cubby, which was right next to Janey's. Janey told her friend what she'd just found out from Leah.

"That's too bad," Lolli said. "Leah must be so worried."

"She is. And so am I." Janey noticed that Lolli didn't seem to be listening very carefully. She was looking at something over Janey's shoulder. When Janey looked that way, all she saw was one of their classmates, a girl named Brooke.

"Have you noticed that Brooke doesn't seem like her normal self?" Lolli whispered.

"Not really," Janey said. "What do you mean?"

"She's usually so happy and outgoing.

But lately she's been a lot quieter. Today it even looks like she's been crying!" Lolli took a step toward Brooke. "I think I'll go ask her if anything's wrong."

"Wait!" Janey said. "We need to figure out what to do about Sunny."

It was too late. Lolli didn't hear her, because she was already hurrying toward Brooke. Letting out a sigh, Janey followed.

"Hi, Brooke," Lolli said when she reached the other girl. "Are you okay?"

Brooke was short with long, black hair. Right now her hair was hanging over her face, hiding one of her brown eyes. But the eye Janey could see looked sad.

"I'm fine," Brooke said.

"Are you sure?" Lolli put a hand on Brooke's arm. "You seem kind of upset

164

or something. If you need someone to talk to…"

"No, really, I'm fine." Brooke said again. "I have to go."

Grabbing one more book out of her cubby, she rushed off. Lolli and Janey stared after her.

"She's definitely not fine," Lolli said. "Should we follow her and try to talk to her again?"

"Veto," Janey said. "We're supposed to be helping pets, not people, remember?"

Just then Zach zoomed up to the girls on his skateboard. "Hi," he greeted them breathlessly.

"You're not supposed to ride your skateboard in the halls," Janey reminded him. "Don't let the teachers see you, or you'll have to stay after school. And we'll probably need everyone in the Pet Rescue Club to help search for Leah's canary again today."

"Never mind that bird," Zach said. "We need to help Hall Cat. I found her outside again this morning."

He told Janey and Lolli what the neighbor had said. Lolli shook her head.

"I was hoping they'd let her come back inside after we talked to the baby's mom yesterday," she said. "I guess not."

"We need to convince them to take better care of Hall Cat," Zach said. "Or else she might get hit by a car or something!"

"I'm sure her owners don't want that," Lolli said. "They seem nice. Just kind of busy with the new baby."

Janey nodded. "Okay, we should

definitely figure out a way to help Hall Cat," she said. "But what about Sunny? If a cat is in danger outside, what about a tiny little bird? I think we need to find him first, then come up with a plan for Hall Cat."

"No way," Zach said. "Hall Cat needs us right now!"

"Wow," Lolli said. "Now that we started the Pet Rescue Club, there are even more pets to help than I expected! I guess we need to figure out how to help two pets at once."

"Hall Cat will be fine for a few days," Janey argued. "There really isn't much traffic in our neighborhood."

"What if she wanders off and gets lost, though?" Zach argued back. "Or gets attacked by a mean dog, or eats something she shouldn't? There are some plants and stuff that are poisonous to cats—not just onions, either."

Before Janey could respond, she saw Adam walking toward them with Ms. Tanaka, their homeroom teacher. Ms. Tanaka was young and friendly and smiled a lot, which made her almost everyone's favorite teacher.

"Hi!" Janey called. "How's Truman?"

Truman was the dog that had inspired Janey and the others to start the Pet Rescue

Club. With the help of the local animal shelter, the kids had worked together to save him from a neglectful home and help him find a new home with Ms. Tanaka.

"Truman is great!" Ms. Tanaka said with a smile. "I took him for a nice, long walk after school yesterday."

"That's awesome," Janey said. Hearing how well Truman was doing made her more determined than ever to help more animals starting with Sunny.

Ms. Tanaka waved and headed into her classroom. After she was gone, Janey and the others told Adam what they'd been talking about.

"Okay, it sounds like we have two pets who need our help right away," Adam said. "Maybe we should divide and conquer."

"What do you mean?" Janey asked.

Adam shrugged. "There are four of us," he pointed out. "Maybe Zach should talk to Hall Cat's owners after school, and Janey and Lolli can go look for the lost bird."

"What about you?" Lolli asked.

"I'll come help whoever needs me after I take care of my clients," Adam said.

Janey thought about Adam's idea. It made sense. Zach was too hyper to be much help searching for Sunny, anyway.

"Wait, so I have to go talk to Hall Cat's owners all by myself?" Zach asked. "I was hoping you guys could help me convince them."

"Adam can come help you later," Janey said. "I think his plan could work. Let's do it!"

5

Kitty and Cats

Lolli usually liked school. But that day, she was happy when the final bell rang. She was worried about both of the pets that the Pet Rescue Club was trying to help. Besides, she'd had an idea she wanted to tell Jancy and Leah about.

She walked out of the classroom with the two of them. "Ready to go to Leah's house and look for Sunny?" Janey asked her. "I already called my mom to come and drive us there so we don't have to wait for the bus."

"Actually, I was thinking about something," Lolli said. She turned to Leah. "Did you check with the Third Street Shelter after Sunny went missing? Maybe someone found him and took him there."

"I called them yesterday," Leah said. "Nobody had brought him in yet." She bit her lower lip. "Anyway, I doubt anyone except me could catch Sunny."

Janey nodded. "It's okay. He's probably still in your yard. We'll find him."

Janey sounded very certain. Lolli had heard her friend sound that way a lot. Sometimes it meant that Janey was so busy thinking about her own plans that she wasn't paying enough attention to what other people were saying. So Lolli cleared her throat and talked a little louder.

"Even if nobody could catch him, somebody might call the shelter to report seeing him," she said. "If you want, I'll call home and ask if it's okay for me to walk over there and check."

The animal shelter was only a few blocks from school. Lolli's parents had let her walk there before, so she guessed they would say yes today, too.

"That's a good idea," Leah said. "If someone reported seeing Sunny, it will help us figure out if he's still in my backyard or if he flew somewhere else."

Janey blinked at Lolli. "Oh. Yeah, I guess that's true. Are you sure you don't mind going to the shelter by yourself?"

"It will be fine," Lolli said. "One of my parents can probably pick me up there and drive me over to meet you guys at Leah's house."

She said good-bye to Janey and Leah, then headed for the school office to call home. As she'd guessed, her father said it was okay to walk to the shelter. He promised to meet her there in a few minutes to pick her up.

As she walked down the sidewalk, Lolli spotted Brooke walking just ahead of

her. Brooke's head was down, and her steps were slow.

"Hey, Brooke!" Lolli broke into a jog to catch up. "Wait up. Are you walking toward town, too?"

Brooke stopped and waited. "Uh-huh. I'm supposed to meet my dad at his office," she said. "Why are you walking this way? I thought you lived on a farm."

"I do." Lolli and the other girl both started walking again. "But today I'm going to the animal shelter." She told Brooke about the Pet Rescue Club and their search for Sunny.

"Wow," Brooke said. "That's cool that you guys are trying to help animals."

"Thanks." Lolli smiled at her. "Do you walk to your dad's office every day after school?"

"No, I usually take the bus." Brooke sighed. "But everything is different lately."

Lolli leaned closer. "What do you mean? Does it have to do with why you look so sad?" She reached over and gave Brooke's arm a squeeze. "Sorry, my parents tell me I'm too nosy. I just want to help if I can."

Brooke sniffled. Then she took a deep breath.

"You're nice, Lolli," she said. "I guess I can tell you. My grandpa fell and hurt himself a few weeks ago."

Lolli gasped. "Oh, no! Is he okay?"

"Not really." Brooke shrugged. "I mean, his broken hip is getting better, but he still can't walk by himself or go up and down the stairs. So instead of letting him go home

176

after he got out of the hospital, they sent him to another place."

"Another place?" Lolli wrinkled her nose. "What do you mean?"

"It's called an assisted care facility," Brooke said. "He has to live there while he does lots of physical therapy and stuff. Nobody is sure how long that will take."

"Wow." Lolli thought about her own grandfathers. Her dad's dad sold real estate, and her mom's dad was retired but still played golf or tennis almost every day. "No wonder you're upset."

"Not as upset as my grandma." Brooke kicked a stone on the sidewalk. "She's living in their house all by herself now. She says she's fine, but I can tell she's sad and lonely without Grandpa around."

"Oh, that's terrible." Lolli's eyes filled with tears at the thought of Brooke's grandma being so sad.

Brooke nodded. "That's why I'm going to my dad's office. I'm planning to spend lots of time with Grandma to help her feel less lonely. Dad is going to drive me over there today."

"That's nice. I bet she'll love seeing you," Lolli said. "Let me know if I can do anything to help, okay? I'm good at reading to people if she might like that, or I can bake her some cookies…"

Brooke looked thoughtful. "Grandma can read to herself just fine," she said. "But actually, maybe there is something you can do…"

....

"Kitty?" Lolli stuck her head into the cat room at the Third Street Animal Shelter. "The guy at the front desk said you were in here."

Kitty looked up and smiled, spitting out a strand of blond hair that was caught in her lip gloss. She was the Pet Rescue Club's favorite shelter worker.

"Hi, Lolli," Kitty said. "What brings you here today? I didn't see your name on the volunteer schedule." She winked. "Did you come to adopt another dog to keep Roscoe company?"

Lolli giggled. "I'd love to, but my parents would kill me." She stepped into the room to pet a cute tiger-striped cat that was wandering around while Kitty cleaned out her litter box. "Actually, I'm here on official Pet Rescue Club business."

She told Kitty about Sunny. By the time she was finished, Kitty was shaking her head.

"Sorry, no calls about a loose canary," she said. "I'll be sure to let you guys know right away if I hear anything, though."

"Thanks." Lolli leaned closer to the

cat, who had started purring as soon as Lolli started petting her. "Hey, I remember you from my first day volunteering here," Lolli cooed. "You're so cute! I can't believe nobody has adopted you yet."

Kitty nodded. "Yes, Tigs is adorable," she said. "But she's also ten years old, and unfortunately, most people don't want to take on a cat her age."

"Really?" Lolli couldn't help thinking about Hall Cat. Based on what her owner had told Zach, she was probably at least ten years old, too. "Why not?"

Kitty shrugged. "Older animals have a lot of love to give," she said. "But I guess it makes people sad to think they might not have an older pet for as long as a younger one. I don't know. But a cat of Tigs' age will be lucky if anyone even considers adopting her—no matter how cute and friendly she is."

Lolli nodded, feeling a flash of worry for Hall Cat. Her owners said they weren't planning to take her to the shelter. But what if they changed their minds?

They won't, she told herself firmly. She

was sure they'd decide to keep her—and keep her inside, too. After all, the Pet Rescue Club is on the case!

6

Different Strokes

"How many more clients do you have today?" Zach asked, feeling impatient. "I want to get to Hall Cat's house soon."

He'd decided to wait for Adam before starting his mission. Otherwise, he was afraid he wouldn't know what to say again. And that wouldn't help Hall Cat at all.

"Just one more," Adam said, pointing to a blue house up ahead. "It won't take long, since I just have to walk the dog and not feed it or anything."

"Really? Why, is the dog on a diet?" Zach

grinned.

"Ha ha, very funny," Adam said. "It's because the owners just had twin babies."

"Twins?" Zach made a face. "I hope they're not anything like my obnoxious twin brothers."

Adam smiled. "Actually, these twins are pretty cute," he said. "But the mom has trouble walking the dog with both babies along, and the dad works all day in another town. So they hired me to walk the dog for them, at least until the twins are older."

"Oh." Zach thought about that. It reminded him of Hall Cat's owners, except they hadn't hired Adam to take care of their pet. They'd put her outside instead.

When Adam knocked on the door, a young woman with lots of dark curls and big brown eyes answered. Behind her, Zach could see a spacious living room. Two babies were playing with blocks on the rug. A large, fluffy collie was lying there watching them, but he jumped up and barked happily when he spotted Adam.

"Hi there, Brody." Adam rubbed the dog's ears as it rushed over to greet him. "Mrs. Cooper, this is my friend Zach Goldman. He's helping me today."

"Hi, Zach." Mrs. Cooper smiled as she handed Adam a leash. "Goldman—are you related to Brody's vet, Dr. Goldman?"

"Yeah, that's my mom," Zach said. He was used to having people ask about his mother. Almost all the pets in town went to her veterinary practice.

But he wasn't really thinking about his mom. He was still thinking about Hall Cat. He stared at Brody as Adam clipped the leash onto the dog's collar.

"Hey, Mrs. Cooper," Zach blurted out. "Did you think about making Brody live outside when you had your babies?"

Mrs. Cooper looked startled. Then she smiled and shook her head.

"No, not even for a second," she said, bending over to rub her dog's head. "Brody is part of the family. And in this family, that means living inside!"

"But isn't it a lot of work having a dog and twins?" Zach asked. "What if you trip over Brody or something?"

"I suppose it's a little extra work," Mrs. Cooper said, glancing over at the twins. "We had to make sure to introduce Brody to the babies slowly, and we always watch carefully when he's with them." She shrugged. "Any extra work is worth it, though."

"Come on, Zach," Adam said. "Brody is ready for his walk."

Zach kept thinking about what Mrs. Cooper had said as he wandered along after Adam and Brody. He was glad that Brody had such nice owners. But he was more worried than ever about Hall Cat. What could he and the rest of the Pet Rescue Club do to convince her owners to change their minds about keeping her outside?

∙∙∙∙∙∙∙∙∙∙

"Do you think Sunny joined a flock of wild birds or something?" Janey askcd, peering at a bird perched on a branch overhead.

She was in Leah's backyard. The two of them had been searching for Sunny all afternoon. First they'd looked in the back-yard. Then they'd checked the front yard, and then the empty lot across the street. Finally, they'd returned to the backyard, since that

was the closest to Leah's bedroom window.

"I doubt it," Leah said. "Male canaries are solitary. They like to have their own space."

"Really?" Janey pursed her lips. "Wait. Then why are you so sure he flew out the window?"

Leah shrugged. "I'm not sure. But I haven't heard him in the house since he disappeared. Or heard him singing, either."

"Okay," Janey said. "But if you were a tiny bird, and you were loose in a house with a couple of cats and a loud little kid, wouldn't you keep quiet?"

Leah's eyes widened. "You're right! I barely searched inside at all. I was so sure he flew out the window, I didn't even think about him being in the house."

Janey had been feeling discouraged. But

now she was excited again. She might have just cracked the case of the missing canary!

"Come on, Leah." She headed for the back door. "Let's go search inside now!"

7

The Search Is On

Soon Janey and Leah were searching inside Leah's house. Leah's little brother was taking a nap, and her mother was busy on the computer in the den, so the house was quiet. After a while, the gray tabby cat noticed what the two girls were doing and started following them.

"Scat, Buddy," Leah told the cat. "Trust me, Sunny doesn't want to see you right now."

The cat ignored her, rubbing against Janey's legs. Normally Janey loved cats just as much as she loved all animals. But right now seeing one of Leah's cats made her feel uneasy. Cats liked to hunt smaller animals—including birds. What if Leah's cats decided to hunt Sunny?

"We need to find Sunny fast," she said.

Leah glanced at the cat. "I know. But how? If he's scared and hiding, we might never find him!"

Janey thought for a second. "I've got it," she said. "You told us that Sunny likes it when you whistle to him, right?"

"Right," Leah replied. "It makes him happy, and he usually starts singing." She gasped. "Janey, you're a genius! Maybe if I whistle, Sunny will answer!"

"What are you waiting for?" Janey smiled. She liked being called a genius! "Start whistling!"

They walked around the house slowly, with Leah whistling a merry tune the whole way. Janey listened as hard as she could. Would Sunny answer?

"There!" she cried as they passed an open doorway leading into a bedroom. "I heard something—a whistle!"

"It's Sunny!" Leah exclaimed. She stepped into the room and whistled. Once again, there was a whistle in return!

Janey looked down at Buddy. The cat was still following the girls. He'd stopped and sat down in the bedroom doorway. But he pricked up his ears toward the room and twitched his tail.

Leah stepped into the room and looked around. "I don't see him," she said. "He must

be hiding."

There were lots of places to hide in the room. It seemed to be the place where Leah's family put everything that didn't have another place to go. There were a couple of bookshelves packed full of books and other stuff, a bed with tons of pillows, and lots of other odds and ends of furniture. Several cardboard boxes were stacked in one corner, and the half-open closet door barely contained all the clothes and other things inside. How were they ever going to find a tiny bird in there?

Once again, Janey started thinking hard. She looked around the room and spotted another door.

"Does that door open into your bedroom?" she asked Leah.

"Actually, it opens into the bathroom," Leah said. "I share it with this room—this is just a guest room, so the bathroom is mostly mine."

Janey nodded. Then she bent down and

gently shoved Buddy into the hall. "Sorry, Buddy," she said as she shut the door in the cat's face. "But we don't need your help with this."

"What are you doing?" Leah asked. "Do you have an idea for how to get Sunny to come out? I'm still not sure he'll let me catch him, though." She looked worried. "He must be awfully scared if this is the first time he's sung in two days!"

"Don't worry, I have a plan." Janey hurried over and opened the door into the bathroom. She continued through the small room into Leah's bedroom. When she entered, Buddy was just strolling in from the hall. "Eh, eh, eh!" Janey scolded the cat gently. She scooped him up and deposited him back in the hallway. "Like I just told you, we don't need your help right now."

She closed the bedroom door, shutting the cat out. But she left the doors between the bathroom and the two bedrooms wide open.

"Okay," she said to Leah, who had followed her into her bedroom. "Now we need to put all of Sunny's favorite foods in his cage, and leave the door open. We'll sit very still, and you'll whistle to try to call him in."

Leah nodded. "I get it! We can lure him into his cage. It could work!"

They set Janey's plan into motion right away. Leah filled Sunny's food dishes with lots of tasty treats. Then she and Janey crouched down near the cage.

"Okay," Janey said. "Now, whistle!"

Leah took a deep breath and whistled

her song. At first nothing happened. Janey started to feel worried. What if Sunny couldn't hear them from the other room?

She shifted her weight. Sitting still and being quiet weren't Janey's favorite things. But she knew that if she moved at the wrong time, she might scare Sunny. So she did her best to act like a statue.

"I don't know if this is going to work," Leah whispered. "I don't hear any—wait! There he is!"

Janey heard it, too. Sunny was singing again! And he sounded closer!

"Keep whistling," she whispered. "I think he's in the bathroom now!"

Leah nodded and whistled her song again. Sunny didn't answer this time. But a moment later Janey saw a flash of bright yellow zip in through the bathroom door. It was Sunny! The little canary flew over and perched on top of his cage.

Janey held her breath. Beside her, Leah stopped whistling. Janey could see that the other girl's fingers were crossed, and she guessed that they were both thinking the same thing. Would Sunny go back into his cage?

The next few minutes seemed to last about forty-two days, at least to Janey. But finally, Sunny hopped down onto the top of his cage door. He perched there for another few seconds, then flew right into the cage!

"Oh, Sunny!" Leah cried as she leaped up and snapped the door shut. "It's so good to have you home!"

The little bird pecked at his food. Then he let out a trill before going back to eating.

Janey grinned. "We did it!"

"You did it." Leah spun around and hugged her. "Thank you so much! I don't know what I would have done without you."

"It was nothing," Janey said modestly. "Just another successful case for the Pet Rescue Club."

8

Zach's Mission

"A toast to Janey!" Lolli cried, lifting her bottle of juice.

"And the Pet Rescue Club!" Adam added.

"And the Pet Rescue Club," Lolli agreed.

"Thanks, guys," Janey said with a smile. It was the next day at lunchtime. The four members of the Pet Rescue Club were sitting together in the school cafeteria. Janey, Lolli, and Adam had been sitting together since the beginning of the year. Zach used to sit at a different table. Now he sat with them every day.

Usually there was no forgetting that, since he never stopped talking and joking around. But today he was being very quiet.

"What's wrong, Zach?" Janey asked, giving him a poke on the arm. "Aren't you excited that we helped another pet?"

Zach looked up. "Hip hip hooray," he said with a shrug. "I'm glad you found Leah's bird. But we haven't done anything to help Hall Cat yet."

Adam sipped his chocolate milk. "Yeah, it's too bad her owners weren't home yesterday when we went there."

"We'd better try again today," Zach said. "Let's meet up and go over there right after school."

"Veto," Janey said. "You guys can go without me. I have to stay after school today for my flute lesson."

"Sorry, Zach, but I can't make it today, either," Lolli said. "I promised Brooke I'd take Roscoe to visit her grandma."

"Oh, right," Janey said. Lolli had told the whole group about her talk with Brooke. When Lolli had offered to help, Brooke had explained that her grandmother was a lifelong animal lover. Since Lolli was a member of the Pet Rescue Club, Brooke had asked if she knew any animals who could visit the old lady to cheer her up. Lolli had immediately volunteered to take her own dog, who was super friendly and loved going to new places.

Adam smiled. "The Pet Rescue Club is already expanding," he said. "We started off as people helping animals. Now we're also animals helping people!"

Janey giggled. Adam didn't joke around nearly as much as Zach did, but the jokes he made were usually really funny.

"I guess that's true," Janey said. "After all, Roscoe is an honorary member, since he's one of our mascots. Maybe next time Mulberry can go for a visit!"

She glanced at Zach to see what he thought of that. But he didn't even seem to be listening.

He was looking at Adam. "I guess you can't come to Hall Cat's house right after school, either, right?" he asked. "You probably have to take care of your clients."

"Right," Adam said. "I can come meet you when I'm finished, though."

Lolli nodded. "I probably won't be at

Brooke's grandma's house for that long," she said. "I'll come help with Hall Cat after I'm done, too."

"Me, three," Janey said. "I'll get my mom to drop me off there after my lesson."

"Okay." Zach looked a little happier. He reached for Janey's last carrot stick and popped it into his mouth. "You weren't going to eat that, were you?" he mumbled.

Zach stared out the living room window. He could see Hall Cat's house from there. He could also see Hall Cat. She was sleeping in her owners' driveway. Zach winced every time a car drove by, even though the cat wasn't that close to the road at the moment. But what if she decided to take a nap in the middle of the road next time?

Zach wondered how much longer it would be before his friends showed up. He'd lost his watch weeks ago, so he jumped up and hurried into the kitchen to check the clock on the microwave.

"No way!" he said out loud. He glanced at his oldest brother, who was fixing a sandwich. "Is that clock right?"

Josh glanced at him. "Why? Do you have

an important business meeting?" Snorting with laughter, Josh picked up his sandwich and loped out of the kitchen.

Zach gritted his teeth. The clock had to be wrong! It was impossible that he'd only been home from school for half an hour. That meant his friends probably wouldn't be there for almost another hour!

He hurried back into the living room and looked outside. Hall Cat had woken up. She was sitting up and washing her paw.

"I can't wait any longer," Zach muttered. Yelling to his father that he was going out, he hurried across the street.

This time the baby's father opened the door again. His wife was sitting in a chair right behind him, trying to squeeze the baby's chubby foot into a tiny sock.

When the father saw Zach standing there holding Hall Cat, he sighed. "Hello again," he said. "Is Hall Cat getting into trouble?"

"Not yet," Zach said. "But she might if you keep putting her outside." He took a deep breath, trying to remember all the stuff Janey and the others had said, along with everything his mother had told him about outdoor cats when he'd tried to convince her that Mulberry wanted to go outside and chase mice. "She probably won't live as long being an outdoor cat. She could get hit by a car, or eat something poisonous, or get attacked by mean dogs or wild animals, or—"

"All right, all right," the father said. He sounded a little worried. "I know it's not ideal. But this is a safe neighborhood, and we're just trying to come up with a solution that works for everybody."

Zach took a step inside and set Hall Cat down on the floor. She wandered toward the baby and sniffed at his foot, which was dangling off the side of the chair.

"Careful, Hall Cat," the mother said. "Don't scare the baby." She glanced at her husband. "Put the cat back out, will you, honey?"

Zach didn't think the baby lookcd scared at all. He wondered if the woman had heard anything he'd just said. Zach's older brothers ignored him all the time, and Zach hated it. He was getting the same feeling now.

"Hall Cat's not scary, but I am!" he blurted out. Putting his thumbs in his ears, he waggled his fingers and made a funny

face at the baby. "Ooga booga!"

He was only joking around, but the baby's face scrunched up. A second later he let out a loud wail.

"Oh, no!" the baby's mother exclaimed, grabbing him and hugging him close. "It's okay, sweetie. Don't cry! Please, don't start crying again!"

"I'm sorry." Zach immediately felt guilty. "I was just kidding around. I didn't think that would actually scare him."

The father put a hand on his shoulder. "I know, kiddo. You couldn't know that the baby was up all night with an earache. We're all a little touchy right now, that's all."

"Sorry," Zach muttered again, feeling his face go red. "I guess I'll go."

The mother glanced up at him. "Yes, maybe you'd better," she said with a sigh. "Please take Hall Cat back outside on your way, all right?"

9

Roscoe Helps Out

Lolli was having a great time at Brooke's grandmother's house. Her father had met her in the car with Roscoe right after school. He'd dropped Lolli, Brooke, and Roscoe off at a tidy two-story house just a few blocks from Zach's place.

"Grandma's expecting us," Brooke had told Lolli as Mr. Simpson drove off. "She can't wait to meet Roscoe. She hasn't had a dog in a few years, but she loves them."

Brooke was right. Brooke's grandmother had been thrilled to see them—especially

Roscoe.

"Oh, aren't you a big lug of a fellow?" she'd cooed, walking out onto the front stoop to rub Roscoe all over. The dog had enjoyed every second of the attention, wiggling from head to foot with his tail wagging nonstop.

Finally the old woman had glanced up with a smile. She looked like an older version of Brooke, with friendly brown eyes behind wire-rimmed glasses.

"I'm sorry, where are my manners?" she'd exclaimed, ushering Lolli, Roscoe, and Brooke into her house. It was nice and cool inside, with lots of framed family photos decorating the walls and the scents of lavender and lemon in the air. "You must be Lolli. It's lovely to meet you. You can call me Grandma Madge if you like."

"Okay." Lolli smiled back, liking the woman already. "It's nice to meet you, too, Grandma Madge. This is Roscoe."

"Oh, I know." Grandma Madge rubbed the dog's ears. "Brookie told me all about both of you. Is it true you live on a farm?"

"Yes," Lolli said. "It's not a very big farm, but it's big enough for the three of us. My parents grow all kinds of organic vegetables, and sometimes they make cheese from our goats' and sheep's milk."

"Wonderful! Roscoe must love having a whole farm to patrol," Grandma Madge said.

Brooke flopped onto a comfortable looking sofa. "Grandma loves big dogs," she told Lolli. "Isn't that right, Grandma?"

"Absolutely." Grandma Madge sat on a chair and patted her knees. Roscoe came over and laid his big, blocky head on the woman's lap. His tongue flopped out, and drool dribbled onto Grandma Madge's slacks.

"Oops," Lolli said. "Sorry about that. He drools when he's happy."

"Oh, don't be silly." The old woman

laughed. "What's a little drool among friends? Why, I once had a Saint Bernard who could sling drool farther than you could toss a ball…"

After that, she was off and running, telling the girls a whole series of stories about the dogs and cats she'd known throughout her long life. She'd always had at least one pet around for as long as she could remember.

"…and of course, Brookie remembers Muffin," she finished, glancing at her granddaughter.

Brooke nodded. "She was this awesome dog Grandma had when I was little," she told Lolli. "Muffin used to let me dress her up, even though she was even bigger than Roscoe."

Lolli laughed. "She sounds cool," she said. "What kind of dog was she?"

"Nobody was ever quite sure." Grandma Madge chuckled. "She was just this gorgeous big black-and-tan mixed breed who could shed enough fur in a week to make three new dogs. We used to take a survey at parties to see what mix of breeds people thought she might be. We got everything from Great Dane to German shepherd to giant schnauzer!"

"Whatever breeds she was, Muffin was the best," Brooke said.

"Yes, she was quite a dog," Grandma Madge agreed with a faraway look in her eyes. She rubbed Roscoe's ears. "She passed on a few years ago now."

"Did you think about getting another

dog?" Lolli asked. "Or did you miss Muffin too much?"

"Oh, I missed her all right. And yes, I thought about getting another. But by then, I was feeling too old to handle another large dog."

"I tried to talk them into getting a smaller dog, like a beagle or something," Brooke put in. "Or maybe a cute little kitten from the shelter."

Grandma Madge nodded. "We did consider it, but my husband was starting to get unsteady on his feet around that time. It just didn't seem worth the risk of him tripping over a new pet." She sighed. "Plus, I'm not sure I have the energy anymore for a lively puppy or kitten."

"That's too bad," Lolli said. "I can't

imagine not having animals around." She thought about Leah's pet canary. "Did you think about getting a pet that doesn't run around the house?"

"You mean like a bird or something?" Grandma Madge shrugged. "That just wouldn't be the same."

She looked sad for a moment. Then Roscoe reached up and slurped her face with his large tongue, knocking her glasses askew.

"Oh!" Lolli exclaimed as she reached for her dog. "Roscoe, no! Bad dog!"

But Grandma Madge was laughing as she took off her glasses and rubbed them on her shirt. "No, don't scold him," she told Lolli. "He's just doing what dogs do. And I love it!" She stuck her glasses back on and stroked Roscoe's head.

Lolli smiled, though she felt a little bit sad herself. Grandma Madge loved animals— that was obvious. It was too bad she'd been without a special pet of her own for so long.

But thinking about Leah's bird had reminded Lolli about the Pet Rescue Club. That made her remember that she'd promised to meet her friends to talk to Hall Cat's owners. She stood up.

"I'm sorry, I should probably go," she

told Grandma Madge and Brooke. "But maybe Roscoe and I could stop by and visit again another time?"

"I'd love that." Grandma Madge hugged Roscoe. "Please, come by whenever you like." She winked. "You too, Lolli."

Soon Lolli was hurrying down the sidewalk. "I wonder if the others are already at Hall Cat's house," she said to Roscoe. "Should we go to Zach's house first to see if he's there, or..."

She let her voice trail off. Just ahead, Hall Cat's front door had just swung open. A second later, Zach stepped out, looking red-faced and upset as he clutched Hall Cat in his arms.

10

Lolli's Big Idea

"Zach!" Lolli rushed over as Zach stumbled toward the sidewalk, still holding Hall Cat. "What happened? Where are the others?"

"Not here yet," Zach said. Then he blinked. "Wait, yes they are."

Lolli looked around. Adam was hurrying down the sidewalk toward them. Janey was just climbing out of her mother's car at the curb.

"Sorry I'm late," Adam said breathlessly. He looked at Hall Cat. "Did you talk to her owners?"

"Sort of," Zach said.

Janey rushed up. "Hi, Roscoe," she greeted the dog as he jumped around happily. "What's going on, you guys? Oh! Hall Cat is still outside."

Zach nodded. "I tried talking to them," he said. "They didn't listen."

"Why didn't you wait for us?" Janey said. "Come on, let's go try again."

"I don't think that's a good idea." Zach stroked Hall Cat's back, making her purr. "They seem kind of, um, distracted right now."

Adam shook his head. "It seems like those people just don't have time for a pet," he said. "Cats are a little easier to take care of than dogs. But cats need attention, too!"

"I know, right?" Zach tickled Hall Cat

under her chin. "Especially Hall Cat. She's so sweet! I wish I could take her home. I bet they would let me." He sighed. "Unfortunately, my parents definitely wouldn't let me."

Lolli stared at Hall Cat. Then she stared at her friends. She was starting to get an idea...

"I wish I could take Hall Cat home, too," Janey said. "But you know about my dad's allergies. Maybe you could take her, Adam?"

"Sorry, I can't," Adam said. "My family's landlord doesn't allow any pets. That's why I don't have a dog, remember?"

"Really?" Janey blinked at him. "Oh. I never knew that."

Zach rolled his eyes. "That's because you never stop talking long enough to listen to anybody else."

Janey looked wounded. "I do too!"

"Don't start arguing," Adam told them. "We're supposed to be figuring out a way to help Hall Cat, remember? Maybe Lolli could take her home. Her parents wouldn't even notice another animal on the farm, right?"

Zach brightened. "That's a great idea!"

"Lolli?" Janey poked Lolli on the shoulder. "Why aren't you saying anything?"

"I'm thinking," Lolli said. "I might have an idea for a way to help Hall Cat."

"Really?" Adam said. "You mean you thought of something to convince her people to keep her inside?"

Lolli shrugged. "No," she said. "But maybe that's not the point. Even if they kept her inside, they just don't seem that interested in her anymore."

"So you're going to ask your parents if

you can keep her?" Zach asked.

"Me? No." Lolli smiled. "But I might know someone who would appreciate her a lot more than her owners do."

"Really? Who?" Janey asked.

Lolli pointed down the block. "Brooke's grandma," she said. "She loves animals, but she can't have a big dog or a hyper puppy or frisky kitten."

Zach glanced down at the cat purring in his arms. "Hall Cat isn't hyper."

"Right." Lolli smiled. "Come on, let's go ask her owners if they'd be willing to give her up to a good home."

When the baby's father answered the door, he looked annoyed at first. But when he heard the kids' question, he looked thoughtful.

"Do you really know someone who wants Hall Cat?" he asked, leaning down to give Roscoe a pat.

"We're not sure yet," Lolli said. "We need to ask her. But we wanted to get permission from you first."

The man reached out and scratched Hall Cat under the chin. "I suppose that would be all right," he said. "She deserves more attention than we have to give her right now. And I was thinking about what you kids were saying about her being safer living indoors. I'll miss her, though."

"You can still visit her," Janey told him. "The lady who might want her lives nearby."

"We'll come back and let you know what she says," Lolli promised.

Lolli led the others back to Grandma Madge's house. Brooke answered the door when they knocked. She looked surprised to see them.

"Oh," she said. "It's the whole Pet Rescue Club! Is that an animal you're rescuing?" She reached out to pat Hall Cat.

"Maybe," Lolli said with a smile. "Is Grandma Madge around?"

"I'm here, I'm here." Grandma Madge hurried up behind Brooke. "Oh! What a cute kitty. I've always loved black cats!"

Lolli traded a smile with her friends. "We're glad to hear that," she said. "Because Hall Cat happens to be looking for a new home."

Janey nodded. "She's super friendly."

"And she's not hyper," Zach added. "I doubt she'd ever trip anybody, no matter what her owners say."

Grandma Madge looked a little confused. "Her owners?"

Everyone started talking at once, telling Grandma Madge all about Hall Cat. Meanwhile Hall Cat herself started to wiggle in Zach's arms. He set her down on the stoop. Roscoe leaned forward to sniff at the cat, and she batted him on the nose with her

paw. Then she strolled forward between Brooke and Grandma Madge—right into the house!

"Look," Janey said with a laugh. "She's making herself at home already!"

"You little rascal," Grandma Madge exclaimed. She picked up the cat, who immediately started purring. "Oh my, you are a cutie, aren't you?"

"I think she likes you," Lolli said.

Grandma Madge smiled down at the cat.

"Yes. Well, I really wasn't planning on getting a pet. But…"

Lolli held her breath. Would Grandma Madge agree to take Hall Cat?

"You need company right now, Grandma," Brooke spoke up. "Maybe a cat like this would be perfect."

"Oh, I don't know, Brookie." Grandma Madge was still smiling. "I don't think I could ever live with a pet named Hall Cat."

"You—you couldn't?" Lolli's heart sank.

"Absolutely not." Grandma Madge winked at her. "The first thing I'll have to do is come up with a much nicer name."

It took Lolli a second to realize what she was saying. Then she heard Zach gasp.

"You mean you'll take her?" he asked.

"Why not?" Grandma Madge said. "As Brookie says, I could use the company. Until Roscoe came to visit, I didn't realize how much I'd missed having an animal around the house. And a nice, quiet older cat will be much easier to manage than a dog or a younger animal, especially once Grandpa comes home."

"Hooray!" Lolli cried. "Now the only thing left is to decide what to name her!"

"How about Halloween?" Zach said.

"Veto," Janey declared. "That's a goofy name. Why not just call her Hallie?"

"Hallie," Grandma Madge said thoughtfully. "You know, I think I like that."

"We should go back and tell her old owners the good news," Janey told her friends.

"Don't bother," Grandma Madge said, cuddling Hall Cat. "I know the young couple you mean. I'll walk down there myself and let them know." She smiled. "I've been wanting to see that sweet baby of theirs, anyway."

"Awesome!" Janey said. "I guess it's another happy ending for the Pet Rescue Club."

"This totally rules!" Zach exclaimed.

"Yeah," Adam agreed.

Lolli didn't say anything for a second. She was so happy she thought she might burst. The Pet Rescue Club had helped another animal! Better yet, they'd helped a person at the same time! She was sure Grandma Madge and Hall Cat—no, Hallie—would be much happier now that the Pet Rescue Club had helped them find each other. She was pretty sure the baby's family would be happier, too.

"This is definitely a happy ending," Lolli said. "For everyone!"

Meet the
Real Hallie!

Hall Cat, the kitty in this story, was inspired
by a real-life animal rescue story. A black cat
named Hallie was left at a shelter in Illinois
when she was ten years old. Her previous
owners said they didn't have time for her
anymore. Luckily, she was adopted by someone who appreciates older cats, and has been
a wonderful partner for her new owner ever
since!

Too Big
to Run

Too all dogs, big and small.

—C. H.

1
Clinic Clients

"We're here, we're here!" Janey Simpson exclaimed breathlessly as she rushed into the Park View Critter Clinic. "It's Lolli's fault we're late."

Her friend Lolli Simpson giggled and followed Janey into the vet clinic's cozy waiting room. "She's right, it's my fault. I had to feed the goats and sheep before we came."

Lolli's family lived on a small farm. They had two pet goats and a sheep. One of Lolli's chores was to feed the animals on weekends.

"That's okay," Zach Goldman said.

"Mom's not finished yet anyway."

"Yeah, she has one more patient to see," Adam Santos said.

Zach's mother was a veterinarian who owned the Critter Clinic. She had agreed to drive Zach, Janey, Lolli, and Adam to the animal shelter after she finished with her morning clients.

It was easy to guess who her last patient was, since there was only one animal in the waiting room—a cute little Chihuahua. He was wagging his tail while Adam petted him.

"This is Pepper," Zach told Janey and Lolli. The little dog barked when Zach said his name.

"Aw, he's adorable!" Janey perched on the edge of one of the waiting room chairs and rubbed Pepper's head. He licked her hand with his tiny pink tongue and wagged his tail even harder.

The Chihuahua's owner smiled. She was a tall woman a little older than Janey's mom. "Thanks," she said. "He loves everyone. That's why he makes such a good therapy dog."

"Therapy dog?" Janey echoed, a little confused. Pepper was smaller than most of her stuffed animals! How could he be a therapy dog? "Do you mean Pepper leads blind people around?"

"No, that's a service dog," Adam said. "Therapy dogs are different. Mrs. Reed was just telling us all about it. She and Pepper visit hospitals and nursing homes every week. It makes people feel better when they can interact with a friendly animal."

Adam sounded interested in what he was telling the girls. That was no surprise, since Adam was interested in everything having to do with dogs. He ran a successful dog-sitting business even though he was only nine.

"That makes sense," Janey said. "Being with animals always makes me feel better." She sighed. "Even if it doesn't happen often enough."

"Janey is crazy about animals," Lolli

told Mrs. Reed. "But she can't have any pets because her dad is allergic to anything with fur or feathers."

"Oh, dear." Mrs. Reed looked sympathetic. "Well, at least you have the Pet Rescue Club, right?"

Janey's eyes widened. "You know about the Pet Rescue Club?" she asked. "We're famous!"

Zach laughed. "Not exactly," he said. "Adam and I were just telling her about it."

Janey, Lolli, Adam, and Zach had started the Pet Rescue Club to help animals in need in their town. So far they'd helped find great new homes for several animals, including a dog, a cat, and even a pony.

Janey had been good friends with Lolli and Adam even before starting the Pet

Rescue Club. At first she hadn't been sure Zach would make a good member. She still thought he joked around too much. But he was a computer expert and helped run the group's blog. Besides, he knew a lot about animals because of his mother's job.

"It sounds like you kids have done a lot of good for homeless animals so far," Mrs. Reed said. "Let me know if Pepper and I can ever be of any help."

"Thanks," Lolli said. "How did Pepper become a therapy dog, anyway? Did he have to take special classes? Because I bet my dog would love to visit people—he's super friendly."

Janey gasped. "Oh, you're right!" she exclaimed. "Roscoe would be a perfect therapy dog!"

Zach laughed. "Yeah, except it might be a problem if he tries to sit in people's laps like Pepper does."

"True. He's a little bigger than Pepper." Lolli grinned at Mrs. Reed. "He's part Lab, part Rottweiler, and part who knows what."

"Therapy dogs come in all shapes and sizes," Mrs. Reed replied with a smile. "The only important things are the right kind of temperament and some basic training."

"Really?" Zach looked surprised.

The woman nodded, bending down to pat Pepper. "Actually, I've been thinking about getting a second dog myself, and I was thinking I might look for a larger one this time," she said. "Pepper is perfect for snuggling with elderly folks. But children can be a little too rambunctious for such a small, delicate dog. A medium-sized critter might be better for visiting them."

"I know the perfect place for you to find a dog," Janey exclaimed. "The Third Street Animal Shelter! They have all sizes!"

The other members of the Pet Rescue Club nodded. They all volunteered at the shelter, which had helped them place their very first rescue animal.

"Yes, I was thinking of looking there," Mrs. Reed said.

"We're going there after Mom sees Pepper," Zach told her excitedly. "You could come with us!"

The woman chuckled. "Thanks, Zach. But Pepper and I are scheduled to visit a nursing home this afternoon." She shrugged. "Actually, Pepper and I are pretty busy for the next few weeks. But maybe we'll stop by the shelter next month. I'm sure we'll be able to find our new therapy-dog friend there."

Janey frowned slightly. Next month? That seemed like forever away!

"Are you sure you don't have time to go to the shelter sooner?" she asked. "It's open every day of the week. Even tomorrow—

Sunday!"

Lolli poked her. "Don't be impatient, Janey," she said gently. "Mrs. Reed will go when she's ready."

Janey knew her friend was right. Lolli was always thoughtful and tried to see things from other people's point of view.

But Janey liked to look at things from animals' points of view. "Okay," she said. "The thing is, I just know there are plenty of medium-sized dogs in the shelter that would love a new home pronto!"

"Pronto?" Zach said.

"That's Janey's new word," Lolli told him. "It means immediately."

"Oh." Zach rolled his eyes, then looked at Mrs. Reed. "Janey likes to pick out weird new words and use them a lot."

"Pronto, eh?" Mrs. Reed winked at Janey. "Well, we'll see. Maybe we can find a time to get over there sooner after all—I mean, pronto."

Janey smiled. "I hope so."

Just then the vet assistant poked his head out of one of the doors. "Mrs. Reed?" he asked. "The doctor is almost finished with her last patient. Why don't you and Pepper come into exam room two and get settled. She'll be with you soon."

"Thanks, Russ." The woman stood up and whistled. "Come on, Pepper. Time for your booster shots!"

Pepper looked up, alert. Then he barked and trotted at his owner's heel as she followed the tech into the room.

Janey sighed as she watched them go. "I wish I had a Chihuahua like Pepper," she said. "He's so cute!"

"You wish you could take home every dog you meet," Lolli reminded her with a smile.

"Yeah," Zach said. "Wait until you see the dog in exam room one! You'll definitely want him!"

"Really?" Janey glanced at the closed door to exam room one. "What kind of dog is he?"

Zach and Adam traded a grin. "You'll see," Adam said.

2

Too Big to Run?

Janey wanted to ask more questions. But before she could, the door to exam room one opened. Out walked the biggest dog Janey had ever seen! The dog had floppy ears, droopy jowls, and a sweet expression.

"What in the world is that?" Janey cried loudly.

Lolli giggled. "Is it a dog, or a bear?"

The dog's owner walked out, too. He was a lean young man dressed in shorts and a sweatshirt. He smiled at the kids.

"This is Maxi," he said. "She's big, but

she's friendly—it's okay to pet her if you like."

"Maxi is a mastiff," Adam told the others.

"Oh, right," Jancy said. "I recognize her now from my books. I read that mastiffs are a giant breed—and now I see that it's true!"

Janey loved to read books about animals. She was interested in all kinds of dogs and cats. She'd seen pictures of mastiffs before but she'd never seen one in person. Maxi looked even bigger than Janey expected.

The dog drooled happily and wagged her tail as the kids walked toward her. But when she took a step, she limped a little.

"What's wrong?" Lolli asked. "Is she injured?"

The young man sighed. "Yes, that's why we're here. She's my jogging buddy, and we were on a run yesterday when she started limping. Dr. Goldman says poor Maxi blew out both her knees."

"Ouch." Janey scratched the mastiff's massive head. "That sounds painful."

Just then Zach's mother bustled out from the back room. "Here you go, Matthew," she said, handing the young man a bottle. "I found enough pills to last Maxi through the weekend. If you stop by on Monday after-noon, I'll have the rest for you by then."

"Thanks, Dr. G," Matthew said. "I hope these will make poor Maxi feel better."

"They'll help." Dr. Goldman patted the big dog. "But as I mentioned, I'm afraid the only thing that will really help her long-term is surgery."

Matthew winced. "I know, I know," he said. "I just don't know if I can afford it—at least not anytime soon."

"What do you mean?" Janey asked.

"I just graduated from college," Matthew said with a sigh. "I'm working two jobs to make ends meet as it is. I don't know how I'm going to scrape together enough money for Maxi's surgery!"

"Well, we can try the meds for now and

let her get plenty of rest," Dr. Goldman said. "That should make her feel a little better."

"Thanks, doc." Matthew stuck the pill bottle in the pocket of his shorts. Then he snapped a leash onto Maxi's collar. "Come on, big girl," he said. "We'd better head for home."

"Walking only, remember?" The vet said with a smile. "No jogging."

"Promise," Matthew said. "See you on

Monday, doc!"

The kids gave Maxi a few more pats, and then she and her owner left. Dr. Goldman looked worried as she watched them go.

"Why did you tell him not to jog home?" Janey asked the vet.

"Because Matthew is a serious runner," Dr. Goldman answered. "Unfortunately, mastiffs don't make very good jogging companions. They're too big and heavy to handle that much extra stress on their joints."

Janey was surprised. "Maxi is too big to run?" she said. "I thought all dogs loved running around."

"A gentle lope around the park is one thing," Dr. Goldman said. "But miles every day on pavement is another matter."

Just then Russ stuck his head out into the

waiting room. "Pepper is next, doctor," he said.

"Coming," the vet replied. She glanced at the kids. "Pepper is my last patient of the morning. As soon as we're finished, I can drive you over to the shelter."

"We'll be here, Mom," Zach said.

"Thanks," Lolli added.

The vet smiled and disappeared into exam room two. Zach flopped into one of the waiting room chairs.

"We should have a Pet Rescue Club meeting while we wait," he suggested. "We haven't met any needy pets since we found Lola the pony a new home."

"True," Adam said. "Maybe we should post on the blog asking for our readers to suggest other animals that need help."

"Good idea," Lolli agreed. "Janey, what

do you think?"

"Huh?" Janey hadn't really been listening. She was still thinking about Maxi and her sore knees.

Lolli poked her in the arm. "We said, should we post on the blog to find more animals to help?"

"Haven't you guys been paying attention?" Janey said. "We already know an animal who needs our help. Two of them, actually."

"We do?" Lolli's big brown eyes got even bigger with surprise. "Who?"

"I know," Adam spoke up. "Mrs. Reed's new dog, right?"

"Yes, that's one of the animals I was thinking of," Janey said. "Maybe if we figure out which medium-sized dog at the shelter would make the best therapy dog, she'll adopt it pronto."

Zach nodded. "Okay. Who's the second animal?"

"Maxi," Janey replied. "Didn't you hear what Matthew said? He can't afford to pay for her surgery. Maybe we can help."

"How?" Zach scratched his head. "I just spent all of my allowance on some cool new stickers for my skateboard."

But Lolli was nodding. "I think I know what you're thinking," she said. "We could have a fundraiser!"

"Raise money for Maxi's surgery?" Adam nodded thoughtfully. "That's a good idea."

Janey grinned. "I know. So let's start thinking!"

3

Big Ideas

Janey was still thinking about Maxi as the kids all piled into Dr. Goldman's car a little while later. "You said surgery will fix Maxi's knees, right?" she asked as the vet started the engine. "Then she'll be as good as new?"

"Well, she should be much more comfortable, yes," the vet said. "But if Matthew keeps asking her to run with him, it won't be long until she's right back where she started."

"You mean she'll probably hurt her knees again?" Adam sounded worried.

Dr. Goldman shrugged. "As I said,

mastiffs aren't built for lots of running."

Janey traded a look with her friends. "We should still try to raise money for the surgery," she said.

"Definitely," Lolli agreed. "Matthew will probably stop taking Maxi jogging if he understands it's hurting her."

Dr. Goldman looked at the kids in the rearview mirror. "Raise money for surgery?" she asked. "Is this a new Pet Rescue Club project?"

"Yes," Janey said. With her friends' help, she told the vet about their idea.

By the time they finished, Dr. Goldman was nodding. "I think that's a super plan," she said. "I'll be happy to donate my time free of charge. So you'll just need to raise enough to cover the cost of the surgical supplies and medications."

"Hooray!" Lolli cheered. "Thanks, Dr. Goldman!"

The vet smiled. "You're welcome. So what kind of fundraiser are you planning?"

"We're not sure yet," Janey said. Pepper's appointment hadn't taken very long, so the kids hadn't had much time to talk about ideas. "But I'm sure we can come up with something pronto."

"I hope you have an extra-large operating table, Mom," Zach said with a laugh.

"Yeah." Lolli nodded. "I thought Roscoe was pretty big until I saw Maxi!"

Adam grinned. "She's almost as big as Lola the pony!"

Dr. Goldman chuckled. "Believe it or not, Maxi isn't the largest mastiff I've ever seen. The females are usually a little bit smaller than the males."

··········

They arrived at the shelter. "Call me when you're ready to leave," said Dr. Goldman. "I'll be at the clinic taking care of some paperwork, so I can pick you up whenever you like."

When the kids entered, there were several people in the lobby. Kitty, a worker at the shelter, was handing a piece of paper to an older couple. The husband was holding a crate. A cute dog with a pointy nose was peering out through the mesh door.

"Oh, did Peanut get adopted?" Janey asked, rushing over to peer in at the dog. "That's great! He's an awesome dog."

When Peanut, a dachshund mix with short legs and silky fur, had first arrived at the shelter a couple of weeks earlier, he'd been pretty shy. So Janey spent time with him to help socialize him to new people and situations. He got comfortable and relaxed pretty quickly and then became very friendly and playful.

"We know." The wife smiled at all the kids. "He's a sweetheart."

"Congratulations on the new addition to your family," Kitty said. "Just call us if you have any questions or problems, okay?"

"Thank you." The husband leaned down to look at the dog. "Come on, Peanut. Let's go home."

The couple hurried out. Kitty was still smiling.

"I think Peanut is a perfect match for those two," she said. "They both work from home, so he'll get lots of attention."

"That's great," Adam said. "Peanut is a great dog, but he needed just the right home."

"Yeah." Lolli giggled. "Peanut definitely wouldn't want to live with Matthew, for instance. No way could he keep up with all that jogging on those short little legs!"

"Matthew is a dog owner we just met at the vet clinic," Zach told Kitty. "He's a serious jogger, and he has this huge mastiff named Maxi who runs with him."

"Really?" Kitty looked surprised. "I

didn't think mastiffs made good running companions."

"That's exactly what my mom said," Zach told her. "She says all that running wrecked Maxi's knees."

The other kids joined in to tell Kitty all about Maxi and Matthew and their idea to have a fundraiser for them.

"Wow," Kitty said when they finished. "What a great idea! Why don't you guys brainstorm while you clean some kennels?"

Adam laughed. "Is that your way of telling us to clean some kennels?"

Kitty laughed, too. "Yes, it is. Now get to work, kids!"

"Pronto!" Janey added, which made everyone laugh again.

Soon the four members of the Pet Rescue

Club were hard at work cleaning kennels in the shelter's dog room. It wasn't Janey's favorite job at the shelter, but she didn't mind it too much, because she knew it helped the animals that lived there.

Besides, working in the kennel room gave her a chance to check out the dogs there. "Mrs. Reed wants a medium-sized dog," she reminded Lolli, who was working beside her. "That gives us plenty of choices. There are lots of medium-sized dogs here."

Lolli nodded. "How about Daisy the corgi? She's pretty friendly."

"Maybe," Janey agreed. "Or there's that terrier mix, or maybe…"

She cut herself off as the door opened and Kitty hurried in. "Did you guys finish cleaning out Peanut's kennel?" the shelter worker called. "Because we already have a new resident for it."

"Really?" Janey stepped into the aisle and saw that Kitty was leading a wiggly black dog with perky ears and a long snout.

"Doesn't he have to go in the quarantine room first?" Adam asked.

"The quarantine room is full right now," Kitty replied. "Besides, this dog's former owners brought his vet records. He's up-to-date on everything." She sighed. "They can't keep him because they're moving."

Janey traded a sad look with her friends. She couldn't believe so many people gave up their pets when they moved, or for other reasons that didn't seem very important to Janey.

The dog sniffed at Zach, his tail wagging nonstop. Then he barked and leaped against his legs, as if trying to climb right up into Zach's arms.

Zach laughed and hoisted him up for a hug. "Aw, he's really friendly!" he exclaimed as the dog eagerly licked his face from chin to forehead. "What's his name?"

"Ace," Kitty said. "He's a Lab mix."

"He's small for a Lab mix," Adam commented.

"Yes," Janey said with a thoughtful smile. "I'd definitely call him medium-sized, wouldn't you?"

"I suppose so." Kitty took Ace back from Zach and led him to the empty kennel. "Here you go, boy. I hope you like your new home."

"Don't worry," Janey said, still smiling. "I doubt he'll be there for long."

"Hope not." Kitty headed for the door. "Well, I'd better go finish his paperwork."

She hurried out. Zach kneeled and poked his fingers in through the bars so Ace could lick them. Meanwhile, Lolli stared at Janey.

"Let me guess," she said. "You think Ace should be Mrs. Reed's new therapy dog?"

"He's perfect!" Janey stuck her fingers in beside Zach's and giggled as Ace licked them.

He then leaped away to sniff at his new water dish. "He's definitely friendly, right? And he's medium-sized."

Adam looked dubious as he watched Ace race over to stare at the dog in the next kennel. "He seems pretty hyper," he said. "I'm not sure that's going to work for a therapy dog."

Janey shrugged. "He's just excited to meet us. I'm sure he'll be fine once he has a new owner and a new job as a therapy dog to keep him busy." She straightened up and looked at her friends. "Okay, that's one animal helped!" she declared. "Now let's talk about Maxi's fundraiser."

4
Brainstorming

By Monday at lunchtime, the Pet Rescue Club still hadn't settled on what kind of fundraiser to have for Maxi. They'd been too busy to talk much at the shelter on Saturday. On Sunday, Janey had plans with her family and Adam had several extra dog-sitting clients. So the kids hadn't been able to meet then.

"How about a bake sale?" Janey licked some crumbs off her fingers. "My mom's gardening club had one last year. It was fun."

"A bake sale?" Zach wrinkled his nose. "Sounds kind of girly."

"What's wrong with being girly?" Janey shot back.

"It could be a bake sale where we just sold dog treats, maybe," Adam suggested.

"Do you know how to make dog treats?" Lolli asked.

Adam shrugged. "No. But we could look up recipes on the Internet."

"Sounds complicated," Zach said. "Anyway, buying all those ingredients would be expensive. We'd have to sell a whole lot of dog treats to make enough to pay for Maxi's surgery."

"Maybe he's right." Lolli sipped her drink "We need something simpler."

"And something that will make a lot of money," Janey added.

Adam shrugged. "Okay. What about an auction? We could ask businesses to donate stuff and then auction it off."

"That sounds pretty complicated, too," Zach said.

Janey nodded. "And it would take too long," she said. "Maxi needs help pronto, remember?"

By the time the bell rang to end lunch, nobody had come up with a good plan. Janey felt frustrated.

"We need to think of something," she said. "Let's meet after school."

"I can't," Adam said. "I'm going to the dentist."

"And I told my mom I'd help update the computers at the clinic right after school," Zach said.

Janey frowned. How were they going to help Maxi if they couldn't even find a time to meet, let alone come up with a good idea for a fundraiser? "Okay, what about tomorrow after school?" she said.

"That's fine with me," Lolli agreed.

Adam shrugged. "I only have a couple of clients," he said. "I could meet you guys right after that."

"I'm in," Zach said. "But wait—shouldn't

we tell Matthew about all this?"

"Definitely," Lolli agreed as she gathered up her lunch bag. "Maybe he'll have some fundraising ideas."

"Matthew's supposed to stop by and pick up more medicine today, remember?" Zach said. "Maybe I'll see him while I'm at the clinic."

"If you do, tell him about our plan," Janey said. "In the meantime, everyone keep thinking."

....

After school, Janey and Lolli walked to the animal shelter. Lolli's father had agreed to pick them up there later.

"Is Ace still here?" Janey asked Kitty when they walked in.

Kitty nodded. "Yes, he's here," she said.

"I haven't even had time to put his picture on the website yet."

"We could take his picture if you want," Lolli offered.

"Thanks, that would be great." Kitty reached under the desk for a digital camera. "You could take him for a walk in the court-yard and try to get some pictures there." She laughed. "Good luck getting him to stay still long enough to get a good shot!"

Janey grabbed a leash off the rack near the dog room door. Volunteers at the shelter weren't allowed to take animals off the property without a staff person along. But they could take dogs into the enclosed courtyard at the back of the building.

"Hi there, Acey-Wacey!" Janey sang out as she and Lolli reached the new dog's kennel. "Ready for your close-up? We're going to make you look adorable!"

"I'm surprised you're so excited about taking his picture," Lolli said. "What if someone sees him on the website and adopts him before Mrs. Reed gets to meet him?"

"Don't worry, I already thought of that." Janey opened the kennel door and smiled as Ace rushed out and leaped against her legs. "I'm going to e-mail the pictures we take to Zach's mom and ask her to forward them to Mrs. Reed."

"Oh!" Lolli's eyes widened. "Good idea."

Ace pulled eagerly on the leash as they headed out of the dog room. "Hang on, Ace," Janey said with a giggle. "Wait for us!"

Ace barked and spun around, getting the leash tangled around his legs. Janey untangled it, then hurried toward the door.

The courtyard was small but sunny. It was paved around the outside, but the middle part was grass. The shelter building's walls surrounded it on three sides, with a high brick wall at the back.

Ace barked as he dashed onto the grass. After that, he hardly stopped moving. He leaped up to snap at a passing butterfly, dug

at the ground, and sniffed at everything.

"Wow," Lolli said. "He sure has a lot of energy."

"He'll need it to be a therapy dog," Janey said. "It sounds like Mrs. Reed goes to a lot of places. Now hand me the camera and let's get started on our photo shoot!"

....

"There, that's done." Janey looked up from her tablet computer. "Now let's brainstorm ideas for Maxi."

She was in Lolli's sunny purple-painted bedroom. The two of them had just sent an e-mail to Dr. Goldman telling her about Ace. They'd attached the best pictures from their photo session. A lot of the pictures hadn't turned out very well, since Ace didn't like to stand still. But they'd found a few good ones.

"Okay." Lolli leaned back against her pillows. "We already decided not to do a bake sale. Or a car wash. Or a silent auction." She ticked off each thing on her fingers.

"Right." Janey closed her e-mail. "Maybe we should look for ideas online."

"Yeah." Lolli sat up and leaned closer. "There are probably lots of sites about that."

Janey nodded and typed "raising money to help animals" into a search engine. She scanned the first few items that came up, but nothing sounded too promising.

Then she spotted something farther down the list. "Look at this," she said with a giggle. "It's a site of pictures of cats dressed up like bankers and stuff."

"Ooh, cute!" Lolli grinned. "Let's look."

"Okay—but only for a second. Then we

have to get back to work." Janey clicked on the link.

Forty minutes later, the two girls were giggling over a photo of a cat wearing a ballerina's tutu. Lolli's mother poked her head into the room.

"Janey, your mom's here to pick you up," she said.

Janey gulped. "Oops," she said to Lolli. "I guess we got a little distracted."

"That's okay," Lolli said, though she looked worried, too. "Maybe Adam or Zach has thought of something good."

5

Meeting and Greeting

"Thanks, sweetie." Dr. Goldman leaned over Zach's shoulder and peered at the computer screen. "You've been a lot of help today."

Zach shrugged, spinning around in the reception chair and glancing around the clinic waiting room. "You're welcome. It's kind of fun working here. You know, sometimes."

He was surprised to realize that was true. Up until recently, he'd hated having to spend time at the vet clinic. It smelled like disinfectant, and he wasn't allowed to ride his skateboard in the waiting room even though the tile floor was perfect for it.

But ever since joining the Pet Rescue Club, it hadn't seemed so boring. It was fun to help out with the animals. Besides, his mom paid him extra allowance to keep her computer system up to date. Zach was better than anyone else in the family at computer stuff. Even his older brothers admitted it. And his dad worked at home and was hopeless when it came to technology. He needed Zach's help a lot.

Zach's mother clicked a few keys. "Oh, look, there's an e-mail from Janey," she said.

She opened it. Several photos were attached to the message.

Zach scanned the text. "Oh, right, that's the new dog at the shelter," he told his mom. "Janey thinks he'd be the perfect new therapy dog for Mrs. Reed."

"Yes, I saw that dog this morning," his mother said. "He cut his paw on something and Kitty asked me to take a look."

"He's great, isn't he?" Zach smiled as he remembered how Ace had slurped his face. "I bet Mrs. Reed and Pepper will love him!"

"Maybe." His mother didn't sound too sure. "He seemed a bit, er, lively. But it can't hurt to forward the pictures to her and see what she says."

Zach stretched and stood up. "Do you need me to do anything else?" he asked.

Two Siamese cats were waiting for his mother in one of the exam rooms, and the waiting room was empty.

But it didn't stay that way for long. The door opened, and a woman came in carrying a two-year-old girl in one arm and a large gray tabby cat in the other.

"Hello, Ms. Patel," Zach's mother greeted her. "This is my son, Zach. Zach, this is Ms. Patel and her daughter, Olivia."

"Hi," Zach said.

"Hello, Zach, it's nice to meet you," the woman said. The toddler just stared at Zach and sucked on her fingers.

Zach glanced at the cat. "Your cat looks

sort of like ours, except ours is orange instead of gray. His name's Mulberry."

"This is Toby. He hates being in a crate." Ms. Patel set the cat down. He stretched, then wandered over and meowed at Zach.

Zach laughed and bent down to tickle the cat's chin. "He's talkative."

His mother checked her watch. "You're a little early," she told Ms. Patel. "I'll be with you in a few minutes, all right?"

"No hurry." Ms. Patel spread a small blanket on the floor and set Olivia on it. She dumped a bag of toys beside the toddler, then sat back and sighed. "It feels good to relax!"

Dr. Goldman chuckled, then glanced at the counter. A large pill bottle was sitting there. "Matthew hasn't picked up his meds yet?"

Zach shook his head. He'd been watching for Maxi's owner. "I hope he gets here soon. I want to tell him we're going to help Maxi get her surgery."

His mother nodded, then disappeared into the exam room. Zach sat on one of the chairs. Toby jumped up beside him and started purring.

"He's really friendly," Zach said, petting the cat and watching Olivia play with some plastic blocks. "Hey, I wonder if cats can be therapy animals, too? Maybe Mulberry could do it."

"Therapy animals?" Ms. Patel echoed.

"Yeah." Zach smiled as Toby head-butted him. "I know this lady who takes her dog to nursing homes and stuff to visit people."

"Oh, yes, I've heard about that." Ms. Patel

nodded. "My husband's father is in a nursing home, and he loves when animals come to visit."

Before Zach could respond, the clinic's front door opened. Maxi walked in, followed by Matthew. Olivia's eyes widened.

"Doggy!" she shrieked loudly.

Maxi pricked her ears. "Oh, dear," Ms. Patel said, bending to pick up her daughter. "What a large dog! Watch out, Toby."

"It's okay," Matthew said. "Maxi loves kids and cats. She's great with my nieces. And she plays with my neighbor's cat, Ralphie. Maxi's big, but very gentle."

Zach stepped over and gave Maxi a head rub. "Hi again, Maxi. How are your knees feeling?"

Matthew smiled, but he looked worried. "The medicine makes her feel better, but she's still limping a little." He sighed. "That's why I'm so late getting here. I just got off work, and since Maxi can't run with me right now, I figured I'd walk her here so we'd get to spend a little time together."

"Is she really gentle?" Ms. Patel asked. "I think Olivia would like to say hi."

Zach glanced at the toddler. She was wiggling in her mother's arms, reaching out toward the big dog.

"She's fine." Matthew smiled. "Come here, big girl. Sit."

Maxi sat at Matthew's feet, her tongue lolling out as Ms. Patel stepped toward her and put Olivia down. The little girl cooed and grabbed at the big dog, patting her on the head with both hands.

"Gently, Olivia," Ms. Patel said. "Just like when you pet Toby."

Olivia giggled and tugged on the dog's ear. Maxi looked surprised, but didn't move. Matthew laughed.

"Good girl," he said, rubbing her head. "See? I told you—she loves kids."

Zach grinned. "I think someone else wants to meet her." He pointed at Toby, who was sniffing cautiously at Maxi's tail. When the dog wagged it, the cat leaped back and hissed.

"Oh, Tobes." Ms. Patel chuckled. "He's not used to dogs."

Suddenly Zach remembered the medication. He grabbed the bottle. "Here," he said, handing it to Matthew. "Mom said to give you these."

"Thanks." Matthew pocketed the bottle of pills. "I hope they help."

"Yeah. But surgery will help more, right?" Zach said. "My friends and I had an idea about that. We want to have a fundraiser to pay for it!"

"What?" Matthew looked startled. "What do you mean?"

Zach told him about the Pet Rescue Club.

"So this is our new project," he finished with a grin. "Helping Maxi!"

"Wow!" Matthew grinned back. "That's amazing! Are you sure you guys want to do this?"

"I think it sounds like a wonderful idea," Ms. Patel put in. She was stroking Maxi's head while Olivia patted the big dog's side. Maxi was sitting quietly, her tongue lolling out of her mouth. Zach was pretty sure she was enjoying the attention.

"Okay." Matthew scratched his head, still looking stunned. "I mean, I wish I could pay for it myself. But if this is the fastest way to get Maxi feeling better…"

"It is," Zach assured him. "We aren't sure what fundraiser we're doing yet, though, so let us know if you think of any good ideas."

"Will do." Matthew looked happy as he leaned down and gave Maxi a big hug. "Did you hear that, girl? You'll be as good as new soon!"

"Yeah," Zach said. "That doesn't mean she can start jogging again, though. Mom says it's not good for such a big dog to put stress on her joints like that."

"Really?" Now Matthew looked less happy. "But I work so much that our daily runs are really the only quality time we get to spend together. I'm not sure how I'll fit everything in if she has to stay home."

"Oh." Zach wasn't sure what to say to that. "Um…"

Just then Russ called Ms. Patel in to the exam room. At the same time, Matthew's cell phone rang. He answered, then waved good-bye to Zach as he headed out with Maxi following.

Zach stared after him, a little worried by what Matthew had just said.

Then he shrugged. They could figure that stuff out later. First they had to come up with a fundraising idea.

6
A Walk in the Park

"Hi guys," Kitty said with a smile as Janey, Lolli, and Zach walked into the shelter the next afternoon. "Where's Adam?"

"He had to take care of some clients right after school," Lolli said. "He's meeting us here in a little while."

Janey nodded, feeling impatient. The group still hadn't come up with a good idea for their fundraiser.

"I hope Adam gets here soon," she said. "We need the whole Pet Rescue Club to come up with the perfect idea."

"In the meantime, why don't you help me walk some dogs?" Kitty suggested. "I was going to take Patch to the park. If you guys come along, we could take a second dog with him."

That made Janey forget about her problems, at least for a moment. "How about Ace?" she asked eagerly. "I bet he'd like some exercise."

Kitty chuckled. "I know he would. But he's not quite ready to walk in public yet," she said. "We're still working on his leash manners. Besides, one of the other workers took him out for some exercise earlier. Apparently, he tossed a ball for Ace for almost an hour and Ace never got tired."

Zach laughed. "Yeah, that sounds like Ace." He glanced at Janey. "That reminds me.

My mom got those pictures you guys sent her yesterday."

"Great!" Janey said. "Did she forward them to Mrs. Reed?"

"I think so." Zach shrugged. "Mom wasn't sure Ace would be a good therapy dog, though. He's too hyper."

Janey frowned. "He's not that hyper. Anyway, I'm sure Mrs. Reed can handle him."

"Do you know someone who might want to adopt Ace?" Kitty asked. "That would be great. He's not a dog who would work for just anyone. He'll definitely need a special home."

"Mrs. Reed is definitely special," Janey said. "I sent some pictures to her. I'm sure she'll love Ace."

"Great." Kitty checked her watch, sounding distracted. "Come on, we'd better get moving."

A few minutes later the four of them left the shelter. Kitty was holding a leash attached to Patch, a scruffy looking terrier cross. Janey was walking an apricot-colored miniature poodle named Peaches.

"Follow me," Kitty said, setting off along the sidewalk. "What a nice day!"

Janey nodded. It was warm and sunny. Lots of people were out enjoying the pleasant weather.

"Look, Mommy!" a little boy cried from across the street. "Doggies!"

The boy and his mother looked both ways, then hurried across. "Excuse me," the woman said. "My son loves animals. Can he pet your dogs?"

"Yes, and thanks for asking first," Kitty replied with a smile. "Not every dog is friendly, but these two definitely are. Go ahead, young man."

Mother and son cooed over the dogs for a few minutes. After they moved on, an elderly man stopped to admire Patch, telling a long story about how he had a dog just like him as a child.

By the time the man said good-bye, Janey felt a little impatient. Were they ever going to make it to the park?

Finally they arrived. There were even more people there enjoying the nice day. And most of them seemed eager to come over and pat the dogs. Patch and Peaches both seemed to like the attention.

Not Janey, though. She wished everyone would leave them alone. Maybe then they'd be able to talk about their fundraising ideas.

She sighed as a young woman came over leading a little girl who looked about four. "Hello," the young woman said. "This is Saffron, and I'm Rachel."

"She's my nanny," Saffron informed Janey

and the others. "My mommy and daddy both have very important jobs."

"That's nice," Kitty said with a smile. "Would you like to pet the doggies?"

"Thanks." Rachel smiled back. "She's crazy about animals."

"Good doggie!" Saffron said loudly, lunging toward Patch.

The dog backed off a few steps, looking worried. "Carefully, Saffie," Rachel said.

"Don't scare him."

"Boo!" the little girl yelled, grabbing for Patch again.

This time the terrier-cross dashed behind Kitty to get away. Janey rolled her eyes. Little Saffron might be crazy about animals, but she wasn't very good at petting them!

Meanwhile Saffron grabbed for Peaches. The tiny poodle stood her ground, wagging her tail uncertainly.

"Nice doggie!" Saffron cried, smacking Peaches on the head.

"Oh, dear," the nanny said, yanking the little girl away. "I'm so sorry!"

"Good girl, Peaches," Kitty said, picking up the poodle and cuddling her. Once Rachel had dragged her charge away, apologizing all the while, Kitty glanced at Janey and the others. "Wow, Peaches really handled that well. Maybe she should be your friend's new therapy dog."

"No," Janey said. "Peaches is too small. Mrs. Reed wants a medium-sized dog. Like Ace."

"Oh, okay, too bad." Kitty gave Peaches a kiss on the head and set her down. "Anyway, Peaches shouldn't be too difficult to adopt out. Small dogs are usually easier, especially sweet ones like her."

Zach pointed. "Here come some more fans."

Janey saw a couple of teenage girls coming toward them. "Ugh," she muttered. "Why can't people leave us alone for two seconds?"

Kitty laughed. "Don't be a grump, Janey," she said. "Everyone loves seeing dogs at the park. And we love it, too. The more people who see these dogs, the better their chances of getting adopted."

"Oh, yeah, that's true," Janey said. Suddenly she was glad that Ace wasn't with them. Otherwise he might get adopted before Mrs. Reed ever met him!

Just then Lolli poked Janey on the shoulder. "Look, there's Adam," she said.

Janey looked where her friend was pointing. Adam was coming toward them, walking a sweet-faced collie.

"I know that dog," Zach said. "Adam walks her all the time. Her owner has a really busy job."

"Like Saffron's parents?" Janey said with a giggle.

She expected Lolli to laugh. But Lolli

didn't even seem to be paying attention to Janey's joke.

"That's it!" Lolli cried. "I just had the perfect fundraising idea!"

7

Lolli's Idea

"What is it?" Janey demanded. "What's your idea, Lolli?"

"Yeah, spill it," Zach added.

"Wait." Lolli led them toward Adam. "I want the whole Pet Rescue Club to hear this."

Soon Patch and Peaches were sniffing noses with the friendly collie.

"Hey, guys," Adam greeted his friends. "I just need to take this girl home and then I'll be ready for our meeting."

"Forget it," Janey said. "We're having our meeting right here and now. Lolli just had

an idea."

She crossed her fingers, hoping her friend's idea was a good one. The sooner the Pet Rescue Club settled on a plan, the sooner they could help Maxi!

"Actually, you sort of gave me the idea," Lolli told Adam. Then she smiled at Kitty. "And you did, too."

"What do you mean?" Kitty asked.

"I was thinking about what you said about how everyone likes seeing dogs in the park," Lolli explained. "And then I saw Adam and thought about how people pay him to walk their dogs. That reminded me of the walk-a-thon I did with my parents once."

"A walk-a-thon?" Adam looked interested. "I get it. You want to do a dog walk-a-thon."

"What's a walk-a-thon?" Janey asked. "And how does walking dogs raise any money?"

Lolli patted the collie. "When we did it, we were raising money for an environmental group. My parents and I asked people to sponsor us—that means they promised to pay a certain amount for every mile we walked."

"I get it." Zach nodded. "We could walk dogs right here in the park, and ask people to sponsor us for every mile we go."

"And you could invite everyone in town to walk with their dogs to help raise more money," Kitty suggested. "People love an excuse to get out and do something with their pets."

"So you really think this will work?" Zach asked Kitty.

She smiled and nodded. "It's a fantastic idea," she said. "In fact, if your walk-a-thon is a success, maybe the shelter will do the same thing next year. We're always look-ing for fun ways to raise money—and raise awareness of pets in need at the same time."

"Great." Now Janey was excited. "So how do we get started?"

· · · · · · · · · ·

It turned out there was a lot to do to get ready for the walk-a-thon. On the walk back to the shelter, Kitty gave them some advice. As soon as Adam arrived after dropping off the collie, the Pet Rescue Club got to work. Janey took notes on her tablet computer while the whole group figured out what to do first.

Soon they had a plan to get started. Lolli was going to ask her parents to get permission from the town to hold the dog walk-a-thon in the park. Janey decided to start by designing a poster to hang up at local businesses. And Adam offered to send an e-mail to all the dog owners he knew, asking them to take part.

"What should I do?" Zach asked.

Janey thought for a second. "We need to tell Matthew that we have a plan," she said. "Your mom knows how to reach him, right? Why don't you track him down and talk to him."

"Sure, I can do that." Zach borrowed Kitty's phone and called his mother. She was busy with a patient, but soon Russ arrived to pick him up.

"Where to, Zachie?" Russ asked.

"I need to find Matthew and Maxi," Zach said. "Do you know their phone number? Or where they live?"

"The young man with the mastiff?" the vet tech said. "Actually, I just passed them on my way here."

"You did?" Zach was surprised.

Russ nodded. "Sit tight—let's see if they're still there."

Soon he pulled to the curb beside the local high school's playing fields. Zach spotted Matthew and Maxi right away.

Matthew was dressed in his running shorts and jogging in place on the school's track. Maxi was standing near him, wagging her tail.

"This will only take a second," Zach told Russ. "Can you wait for me?"

"Sure, take your time."

Zach hurried toward Matthew. Halfway

there, he could hear him talking to Maxi.

"No, no, girl," the young man said. "Stay! You don't have to run with me."

"Hey, Matthew!" Zach called. "Hi!"

Both Matthew and Maxi turned. Maxi wagged her tail and hobbled toward Zach.

"It's okay, Maxi," Zach said. "I'll come to you."

He ran faster and soon reached the big dog. As he was patting her hello, Matthew came over, looking worried.

"I thought this would be a good way to spend time with Maxi," he said with a sigh. "If I run on the track, she can hang out in the middle and watch. But she doesn't get it. She keeps trying to run with me, like always."

"She shouldn't do that," Zach said.

"I know, I know." Matthew shrugged. "I

just don't know what else to do."

Once again, Zach was worried. Even if they got her the surgery she needed, would Maxi go back to running and hurt her knees again?

Zach pushed that thought aside. "Listen, I have great news," he said. "We came up with the perfect fundraiser to pay for Maxi's surgery!" He quickly told Matthew about the walk-a-thon.

"That is perfect!" the young man exclaimed. "I did a jog-a-thon once, and it was a blast. Doing it with dogs would be even more fun!"

"Yeah." Zach glanced at the big dog. "But do you think Maxi should walk that far?"

"Probably not," Matthew said with a sigh. "But maybe I can borrow a dog from a friend. I definitely want to help."

"Great." That made Zach feel better. "Tell everyone you can think of, okay? We want lots of people to join in and help us raise money."

"Will do," Matthew promised. He bent down and ruffled Maxi's ears. "Did you hear that, big girl? You're going to get your surgery!"

8

Busy, Busy, Busy

"We need a cute name for our fundraiser." Janey clicked to save the flyer she was designing on her tablet. "Writing 'dog walk-a-thon' on every poster is too long."

Lolli nodded. The two girls were sitting at the big wooden table in Lolli's cozy, messy dining room working on the advertising for the fundraiser. Lolli's mom was on the phone in the next room talking to someone official about reserving space in the park.

"How about calling it, um…" Lolli thought for a second. "The Doggie Dash?"

Janey wrinkled her nose. "That makes it sound like everyone has to run," she said. "I'm not sure it's clear enough, either. We want people to be excited, not confused."

Lolli nodded. "You're right. We should probably have the word 'walk' in the name."

"Walk for Cash?" Janey said. "Or the Dollar Walk?"

"But that's not clear enough either," Lolli said. "There should be something about dogs, or people might think it's a regular walk-a-thon."

"Well, we could put a dog on the poster," Janey said. But she knew her friend was right. "Okay, how about Walk Your Dog Day?"

"I guess that's okay," Lolli said uncertainly.

Janey could tell her friend didn't like her idea—she was just too nice to say so. "We don't want something okay," she said. "We want something great!" She tapped her fingers on the table. "And we need it pronto."

Just then Roscoe wandered over to see what they were doing. He rested his head on the edge of the table, staring at Janey with his big brown eyes.

"What do you think, Roscoe?" she asked, rubbing his head. "You're going to be walking in this thing—what should we call it?"

Roscoe's tongue lolled out, and he wagged his tail so hard it smacked into Lolli's leg. Lolli giggled. "Roscoe wants to call it the Walk and Slobber," she joked.

"No." Janey's eyes widened as the dog's tail smacked her. "Roscoe's a genius! We should call it the Walk and Wag!"

Just then Lolli's mother walked into the room. "The Walk and Wag?" she asked. "Is that what you're calling this thing? I like it!"

"Me, too," Lolli said. And this time Janey could tell she meant it.

"Great!" Janey patted Roscoe. "Thanks for the idea, Roscoe." Then she looked at Lolli's mom. "Did you talk to the park people?"

She smiled. "Yes, and you're on. The Walk and Wag is two weeks from Saturday."

"Two weeks?" Janey pulled her tablet

closer. "Okay, let's get back to work!"

• • • • • • • • • •

"Great poster, kids!" Ms. Tanaka, Janey's homeroom teacher, was holding one of the posters Janey and Lolli had printed out the day before. "I'll hang it right here where everyone can see it."

The entire Pet Rescue Club watched as

the teacher hung the poster in the middle of the classroom's bulletin board. "Will you be in the Walk and Wag?" Zach asked. "You could bring Truman."

Truman was the first dog the Pet Rescue Club had helped. Ms. Tanaka had adopted him from the shelter.

"Truman and I will be there," Ms. Tanaka promised with a smile. "We love to go for walks. A walk for a good cause sounds even better!"

Lolli giggled. "Remember how you wanted a big dog at first?" she asked. "Well, wait until you see Maxi. She's probably the biggest dog in town!"

"Really?" Ms. Tanaka chuckled. "I can't wait to meet her. Now take your seats—it's almost time for the bell."

As the kids hurried to their desks, Janey was still thinking about Truman. Ms. Tanaka had wanted a large dog at first. But it turned out that Truman was the perfect match for her even though he wasn't very big.

I know Mrs. Reed will be the same way, Janey thought. Everyone thinks Ace is too hyper to be a therapy dog. But I bet he'll be a perfect match, too!

· · · · · · · · · ·

"Hi, kids," Kitty said as Janey and Lolli hurried into the shelter lobby the following Friday afternoon. "People have been asking about the Walk and Wag all week!"

"I can't believe it's only a little over a week away." Janey shivered with excitement. "Anyway, I just realized something. Lolli will be walking Roscoe. But I don't have a dog to walk. Can I walk one of the shelter dogs? Maybe Ace?"

Kitty looked thoughtful. "I think we'll have to walk him together, because he's a little too big and strong for you. Okay?"

"Okay!" said Janey. "I bet Adam and Zach will want to borrow shelter dogs, too."

. . . .

By Sunday afternoon, it was settled. Janey, Adam, and Zach were given permission to walk shelter dogs in the fundraiser. The entire Pet Rescue Club visited the dog room to choose which dogs to take.

"What if the dog we pick gets adopted before next Saturday?" Zach wondered, tickling a friendly hound through the kennel door.

Kitty smiled. "I hope we have that problem!" she said. "And don't worry. There are always plenty of dogs here. If yours goes to a new home, you'll just have to choose a different one."

"Which dogs do you think we should pick?" Adam asked Kitty.

"I already picked mine. I'm walking Ace." Janey walked over to Ace's kennel. The lively black dog jumped and barked happily

when he saw her.

"Zach's mom told Mrs. Reed about the Walk and Wag," said Janey. "And she and Pepper are coming. She can meet Ace then."

"Okay," said Kitty. "Anything to help Ace get a good home. He's already had several adopters pass him over."

"Really?" Janey was surprised, but also glad—she didn't want anyone to adopt him except Mrs. Reed. "How come?"

"I know," Zach put in. "Because he's a spaz!"

Kitty laughed. "Well, sort of, yes," she said. "Not every dog is suitable for every type of home. You need to make sure the match is right, otherwise neither dog nor owner will be happy. Ace wouldn't do well with young children, for instance—he'd be too likely to knock them over by accident, just being himself."

"He probably wouldn't be a good dog for my family, either," Lolli said. "He might chase the goats and sheep, or run off if we didn't watch him every second."

Janey looked at Zach, expecting him to make a joke about Roscoe being too lazy to run away. But he looked thoughtful.

"I guess Matthew and Maxi aren't a very good match, either," he said. "Matthew loves to run, but Maxi is too big to run."

"Yeah." That made Janey feel sad for a moment. "I hope he figures out a way to spend time with her that doesn't hurt her knees."

"Let's get her knees fixed first," Lolli suggested. "We can worry about the rest later."

9

The Walk and Wag

"Wake up, sleepyhead. Time to get ready for the walk-a-thon!"

Janey opened her eyes. Her mother was smiling down at her.

"What time is it?" Janey asked with a yawn. Her head felt fuzzy and her eyes so heavy she could hardly keep them open.

"Six o'clock. You told me to wake you, remember? You wanted to have plenty of time to get ready for your dog walk-a-thon."

That made Janey wake up. "Oh, right," she exclaimed, sitting up in bed. "I can't believe it's finally here!"

Twenty minutes later, she was dressed and shoveling cereal into her mouth. Twenty minutes after that, her dad was driving her to the animal shelter.

"Are you sure you have everything you need?" he asked as he pulled to the curb. "If you forgot anything, just call me and I'll run it over to the park. And of course your mom and I will come by later to cheer you on."

"And to pay the money you promised to sponsor me, right?" Janey said.

Her dad chuckled. "Of course!"

The shelter normally didn't open until nine on Saturdays. But today Kitty was already there. So were Dr. Goldman, Zach, and Adam.

"Where's Lolli?" Janey asked.

"She's going straight to the park with Roscoe, remember?" Adam said. "We'll meet her there."

"Oh, right." There were so many details to remember that Janey had trouble keeping track of them all. She looked at Kitty. "Should we get our dogs now?"

"They're ready and waiting," Kitty responded. "I even took Ace for a quick run in the courtyard when I first got here."

"Uh-oh," Zach joked. "I hope you didn't wear him out so he can't walk very far!"

Kitty laughed. "I don't think you have to worry about that. Ace could do this walk-a-thon twice over and still have plenty of energy."

Soon they were all piling into the shelter's van with their dogs. Adam had chosen a terrier mix named Duke, and Zach was going to walk a small dog that looked like a mix of so many different breeds that the shelter had named her Misha, short for Mishmash.

Ace was so excited that he almost pulled the leash out of Janey's hand as he leaped into the van. "Hang on, boy," she said with a laugh. "Wait for me!"

"Be careful not to let him get loose," Kitty told her. "If he does, we might never catch him."

"I'll be careful," Janey promised. She held onto the leash tightly with both hands.

When they reached the park, the work began. Lolli was waiting for them with Roscoe. Her parents were there, too, since they'd offered to help set up for the fundraiser. Lolli's dad watched all the dogs while the others got to work.

There was a lot to do! Before long Janey was out of breath and sweating a little. But it was fun, too. They laid out a course, marking the way with colorful flags. They set up a finish line with bright tape and balloons. Lolli's parents had brought a folding table where people could sign in, and Janey taped the poster she'd made to the front and then carefully set out piles of sign-up sheets and instructions.

By the time everything was ready, people were starting to arrive. A pair of young women walking a pair of pugs hurried over. "Where do we sign up?" one of the women asked.

"Right here," Janey said. "Your dogs are super cute!"

More people were already hurrying over. Janey barely had time to give the pugs a quick pat before she had to get back to work.

··········

"Wow," Lolli said. "I can't believe how many people are here!"

"And how many dogs." Janey glanced around. She and Kitty and Lolli had just started the course with Ace and Roscoe. Lolli's parents and Zach's mom had taken over at the sign-in table so the kids could participate in the walk-a-thon.

"Easy, Ace," Lolli said as the Lab mix leaped up at Roscoe. "Roscoe doesn't want to play right now."

Janey tugged on Ace's leash. The cute

black dog was more excited than ever. He kept trying to dash over to say hi to every dog he saw. And that was a LOT of dogs!

But Janey kept a tight hold on his leash. Kitty walked by her side. Janey also kept a lookout for Mrs. Reed.

"Let me know if you see Mrs. Reed and Pepper," Janey said. "I want to be sure they get to meet Ace."

"Okay." Lolli glanced at Ace, who was straining against his leash and barking at a passing greyhound. "Do you think she'll like him?"

"Of course!" Janey said. "She'll love him. He's medium-sized, right?"

"True," Lolli said. "That part is a perfect match. But like Kitty was saying…"

"Look, there they are!" Janey interrupted.

"Hey, Mrs. Reed! Wait up!"

She hurried to catch up to the woman. Kitty followed them. Pepper saw them coming first and wagged his tail.

Then Ace barked and leaped toward the smaller dog. Pepper jumped back, looking alarmed.

"It's okay, baby." Mrs. Reed scooped up the Chihuahua and smiled at the girls. "Well, hello there! I understand you kids put this whole fundraiser together to help one of Dr.

Goldman's patients. What a wonderful idea!"

"Thanks," Lolli said. "Maxi's owner can't afford surgery, and we wanted to help."

"This is Ace," Janey blurted out as Ace jumped up on Mrs. Reed's legs. "He's the one in the photos we sent. He's, um, a little excited today."

"I can see that." The woman chuckled and let Ace sniff her hand. "Hello there, Ace. Aren't you a lively fellow!"

"Yes, he has lots of energy," Janey said. "That means he could be a good therapy dog, right?"

"A therapy dog? Hmm." Mrs. Reed looked at Kitty. "Maybe if he settles down a bit."

"What do you mean?" Janey said. "I thought he'd need energy to go visit lots of places with you."

"Yes, but many of the people we visit are sick or elderly or both," Mrs. Reed explained. "A dog that's too energetic can be too much for them." She patted Ace. "He's a cute fellow, though. I'm sure he could do lots of things. Maybe dog agility or something like that?"

Janey wasn't sure what to say. This wasn't turning out the way she'd planned at all! How was she going to convince Mrs. Reed that Ace really was the perfect match for her?

··········

"Look! There's Matthew," Adam said.

Zach saw him, too. "Hey, he brought Maxi," he said. "I hope he's not making her run. Or even walk."

"Doesn't look like it," Adam said. "They're just hanging out in the shade talking to people."

The two boys hurried over. "Hi," Zach said. "I thought you weren't going to bring Maxi."

"I couldn't stand to leave her home," Matthew said. "After all, this is all for her! Besides, we haven't been spending enough time together since she had to stop running. I don't want her to be lonely." He gave her a pat. "Anyway, my sister offered to walk with her dog in our place so we could just hang out."

"That's good," Zach said. "Look, I think Maxi likes Misha and Duke!"

The three dogs were circling one another, wagging their tails.

"Oh, Maxi gets along with everybody," Matthew said with a chuckle. "Even tiny dogs can boss her around and she doesn't mind a bit."

Zach nodded, remembering how calm Maxi had been with Toby the cat in the clinic waiting room. "She's pretty chill," he agreed.

"Look," Adam said. "There are Janey and Lolli."

"And Mrs. Reed," Zach added. He waved. "Guys! Over here!"

The girls and Mrs. Reed came toward them. Mrs. Reed was holding Pepper in her arms, while Ace frisked around and barked at Roscoe. Zach noticed that Janey looked kind of grumpy. But she looked that way a lot, so he didn't worry about it.

"This is Maxi," he told Mrs. Reed. "She's the one who's getting the surgery."

"Lovely to meet you, Maxi," Mrs. Reed said. As she leaned down to give the big dog a pat, Pepper wriggled in her arms, sniffing curiously at Maxi.

"You can put Pepper down," Zach said. "Maxi won't hurt him."

"Don't worry," Janey added. "I'll keep Ace away."

"Thank you, dear." Mrs. Reed set the Chihuahua on the ground. Pepper trotted over and sniffed noses with Maxi. Both dogs wagged their tails.

"Oh, and this is Matthew," Lolli added.

"I know." Mrs. Reed smiled. "Good to

see you again, Matthew."

"You too, Prof," Matthew said. Glancing at the kids, he grinned. "Dr. Reed was my professor in college."

"Really?" Zach was surprised. "You're a doctor?"

"A doctor of history," Mrs. Reed said with a chuckle. "Matthew was one of my best students."

As Matthew and Mrs. Reed chatted, Zach wandered over to Janey, who had taken Ace a short distance away. Adam and Lolli came, too. Kitty was sitting on a bench near them, talking on her cell phone to the shelter to see how things were going there.

"What's with you?" Zach asked Janey. "Aren't you having fun?"

Janey shrugged, staring at Ace as he

jumped around playfully with Duke. "I thought Mrs. Reed and Ace were a perfect match," she said. "But Pepper doesn't seem to like him much. And Mrs. Reed thinks he's too energetic to be a good therapy dog."

"Bummer," Zach said. "But don't worry, there are lots of other medium-sized dogs at the shelter. Maybe she'll like one of them better."

He glanced over at Adam to see what he thought. But Adam was staring back toward Mrs. Reed and Matthew. "Do you see that?" he asked.

"See what?" Zach looked where Adam was looking. Pepper was sitting between Maxi's front legs. Maxi was peering down at the little dog, staying very still. Her tail thumped against the ground as she wagged it. Mrs. Reed's hand was resting on the big dog's head, her fingers idly scratching at Maxi's ears as she talked to Matthew.

Zach looked at Adam, who was smiling. "I just had an idea," Adam whispered to him. "Let's go find your mom!"

10
Happily Ever After

By the time she finished the course, Janey was feeling happier. "Are you okay?" Lolli asked. "Even though Ace and Pepper didn't get along?"

"I'm fine," Janey said. "Anyway, it's not hopeless, right? Maybe we should try again on a less busy day. The two of them might get along better then."

Lolli looked uncertain. "Maybe," she said. "But I'm still not sure Mrs. Reed will—"

"Hey!" Adam interrupted breathlessly, jogging up to them with Duke at his heel.

Zach and Misha were right behind them. "We need to talk to you about something."

"What?" Janey asked.

Adam glanced over his shoulder. "Did you notice how well Maxi gets along with little Pepper?"

Janey frowned. Was he trying to rub it in? "Yeah, we know," she grumbled. "Maxi gets along with everyone."

"Exactly." Zach grinned. "And we just checked with my mom— she says mastiffs often make good therapy dogs."

"So what?" Janey said. "Matthew doesn't have enough time to spend with Maxi as it is. How's he supposed to turn her into a therapy dog, too?"

"He's not," Zach said. "Mrs. Reed can do that!"

"Huh?" Lolli blinked.

"It was Adam's idea," Zach said. "He was thinking about how Matthew and Maxi are mismatched."

Adam nodded. "It's like Kitty was saying that time. Some dogs need certain kinds of homes."

"And Matthew's home is the wrong one for Maxi," Zach went on. "Matthew loves to run, and he doesn't have much spare time."

"But running is bad for Maxi." Janey was starting to get it. "So what are you saying? That he should take Maxi to the shelter?"

"No way! He'd never do that," Zach said. "But he might give her to a home that's a better match—especially if he already knows her new owner."

Lolli gasped. "Mrs. Reed!"

"But she wants a medium-sized dog," Janey said. "Maxi is definitely not medium-sized."

Zach shrugged. "She wants a dog that's sturdy enough to visit kids. Maxi definitely is that. And she seemed to like her."

"But what about Ace?" Janey glanced at the black dog, who was trying to convince Misha to play with him.

The two boys traded a grin. "She's a little slow today, isn't she?" Zach commented.

Adam laughed. "Don't you get it?" he told Janey. "We found Ace's perfect match, too—Matthew! He needs a dog that can keep up with lots of running."

Now it was Janey's turn to gasp. "And that's Ace!" She tugged on the leash. "Come on, let's go tell them!"

....

"It's amazing how things worked out, isn't it?" Janey asked Mrs. Reed.

It was a little over a week later and the two of them were in the waiting room of the Critter Clinic, along with the rest of the Pet Rescue Club. Matthew was there, too. So was Ace. The cute black dog was lying on the floor under his new owner's chair, taking a nap.

Janey smiled when she saw that. "I never thought I'd see Ace being so still," she said.

Matthew chuckled. "We went on a nice long run this morning," he said. "He's all tuckered out."

"As they say, a tired dog is a good dog." Mrs. Reed chuckled and patted Pepper, who was sitting on her lap. Then she glanced toward the door leading to the back room, looking anxious. "I wonder how Maxi is doing."

"Don't worry," Lolli told her. "Zach's mom is the best. She'll fix her."

Janey nodded. But she also crossed her fingers. She hoped Maxi's surgery went well so she could begin her new career as a therapy dog.

At first, both Mrs. Reed and Matthew weren't sure about Adam's plan. But the more they discussed it, the more they realized how perfect it was. Maxi would get a good home where Matthew could visit her. He was sad at the thought of giving her up, but happy at the idea that she'd have a job she was good at—being a therapy dog—and would be getting lots more attention, too.

Mrs. Reed hadn't planned on getting such a large dog. But then she decided that size didn't matter. The important thing was Maxi's personality, and that was perfect for therapy work. She was even going to pay for Maxi's surgery herself, so the money from the Walk and Wag could go to the shelter!

As for Matthew, one test run was all it had taken to convince him that Ace would be able to keep up with him.

"It's the perfect happily ever after," Janey murmured as she thought about how well everything had worked out.

Adam heard her and looked over. "Don't jinx it," he said. "It's not happy ever after until Maxi is safely out of surgery."

Janey nodded and stared at the door leading to the clinic's back room. All of them were waiting for the surgery to be over. "Why's it taking so long?" she wondered.

"You don't want Mom to rush it," Zach reminded her.

"I know," Janey said. "But—"

She cut herself off as the door opened and Dr. Goldman stepped out. She was smiling as she peeled off her surgical gloves.

"I won't keep you in suspense," she said. "The surgery went very well. Maxi should recover fully."

"Hooray!" Janey cried, leaping to her feet and doing a happy dance.

That woke up Ace. He leaped to his feet, barking and wagging his tail and doing his own happy dance. Pepper barked, too.

"You said it," Janey told both dogs with a giggle. "Now it really is another happily ever after for the Pet Rescue Club!"

Meet the
Real Maxi!

Maxi, the mastiff who was too big to run, was inspired by a real-life animal rescue story. A mastiff named Millie was given to a mastiff rescue group when she was only two years old. Her knees were injured, just like Maxi's, but a caring new owner adopted her and got her the surgery and care she needed to become healthy again. After that, Millie became a certified therapy dog—just like Maxi!

Kids Getting Involved

Are you a kid who loves animals and wants to help them? Then get involved! Some shelters allow kids to volunteer, like the one in Janey's town. Others only accept adult volunteers for safety reasons. But even if the shelter in your town is the second kind, there are lots of ways to help needy animals. Here are a few ideas:

1. **Organize** a fundraiser for your local shelter or rescue.

2. **Donate** food, toys, or supplies for the shelter pets.

3. **Publicize** your local shelter on your social media channels or just by talking to your friends.

4. **Read** your shelter's website and other animal welfare sites to keep up on current needs and issues and to watch for other ways to help.

5. **Set an example** for all pet owners by always treating your own pet well!

For more ideas, check out:

www.aspca.org

Food for Thought

We share a lot with our pets: our lives, our homes, our love, our deepest secrets. But is it a good idea to share our food?

Not always. Several common foods that are perfectly safe for people can be dangerous or even deadly for our cats, dogs, and other pets. Also, there are some household items and houseplants that pets should never be allowed to chew on or eat. Here are a few examples, but for a more complete list from the experts at the ASPCA®, visit **aspca.org**.

- Onions and garlic
- Chocolate
- Coffee
- Avocado (especially dangerous to birds and rodents)
- Grapes and raisins
- Many human medications
- Antifreeze
- Fabric softener sheets
- Amaryllis
- Pothos (a popular houseplant)

The Right Dog for the Right Home

There are lots of dog breeds out there—and countless adorable mixed breed dogs as well. It can be tempting to choose the cutest dog, or the friendliest, or one that reminds you of a dog from TV or the movies. But it's important to make sure the dog you adopt fits your personality and lifestyle. Do you spend a lot of time outdoors, or prefer quieter pastimes? Do you live in the country or the city? Do you like to keep your house spotless, or will a little—or a lot—of dog hair not bother you? Are you confident enough to handle a dominant breed, or do you prefer someone sweet and easygoing?

All of these questions and more are important to consider. Talk to your local shelter workers about finding the right match, or check out the many resources online to help narrow it down.

Find out more about the ASPCA's "Meet Your Match" program and other great pet information!

(www.aspcapro.org/research/meet-your-match-0)

Good luck finding your perfect pooch—and your happily ever after!

Look for the books in the
PET RESCUE CLUB
series!

1 **A New Home for Truman** 2 **No Time for Hallie**

3 **The Lonely Pony** 4 **Too Big to Run** 5 **A Puppy Called Disaster**

6 **Champion's New Shoes** 7 **A PURR-fect Pair** 8 **Bailey, the Wonder Dog**